The
Boy Next Door

Enid Blyton

The Riddle of the Boy Next Door

AWARD PUBLICATIONS LIMITED

This book was first published in Great Britain
under the title *The Boy Next Door* by Newnes Ltd
in 1944. It was updated and altered to become part
of the Riddle series in 1997 by Enid Blyton's
daughter, Gillian Baverstock.

For further information on Enid Blyton
please visit *www.blyton.com*

ISBN 978-1-84135-742-3

Illustrated by Patricia Ludlow
Cover illustration by Gavin Rowe

First published 1944 as *The Boy Next Door*
Revised edition published 1997 as *The Riddle of the Boy Next Door*
First published by Award Publications Limited 2004 as
The Young Adventurers and the Boy Next Door
This edition entitled *The Riddle of the Boy Next Door*
first published 2009

Published by Award Publications Limited,
The Old Riding School, The Welbeck Estate,
Worksop, Nottinghamshire, S80 3LR

12 3

Printed in the United Kingdom

CONTENTS

Chapter 1

The Boy Next Door

Three children lay under the shade of a large chestnut tree with a golden cocker spaniel panting beside them.

"If only we weren't so far from the village, I'd go and get a huge ice cream," said Laura. "Oh, Russet, I wish you'd blow cold air rather than hot over my legs," she went on, rolling away from him.

"And Aunt Marion's defrosted the freezer so there's no ice cream in the house until tomorrow," said Katie.

"Lazybones, Laura!" said Nick. He scrambled to his feet. "I'll fetch us some ice cream from the village – but you'll have to do the same for me sometime!" He turned away and walked over to the gate.

Katie and Nick were brother and sister. Two years ago, their parents had died in a car crash, leaving them in the care of two guardians. As Uncle Bob, Nick's godfather, had gone to work in Australia, Uncle Charlie, their mother's brother, had agreed to look after them. But his wife, Aunt Margaret, disliked children and did not want Nick and Katie. She was cold, unsympathetic and treated them unkindly. Although Uncle Charlie couldn't bear her constant nagging, he had not stood up for the children against her.

When their aunt threatened to have them taken into care, Nick and Katie had decided to run away. Together with Laura, they made a house in a hollow tree nearby, and Laura and Russet brought them food each day. Eventually they were found when Laura became ill. Mr and Mrs Greyling, Laura's parents, had offered to look after the two children and bring them up with Laura, who was their only child. And although no one would ever replace their own mother and father, Katie and Nick had become very fond of Laura's parents, whom they called Aunt Marion and Uncle Peter.

When Nick came back from the village, all three children sat in the shade and gulped the ice creams down as fast as they could before they melted in the heat. Russet sat hopefully and gazed at each child in turn. Laura gave him the end of her cone, and then turned back to the others.

"Oh, Mum had a letter from Gran and Grandad this morning," she said. "It said that some of the jewellery from the Greylings Treasure had been sold and they have plenty of money now. They want us to go and stay with them again at the end of August."

"That would be brilliant," said Katie. "Greylings Manor is such a beautiful house, and Gran and Grandad are great."

"Whatever shall we do there this time with no mystery to solve?" asked Nick. "It was so exciting following the map to find the Greylings Treasure before that awful man got it!"

"Mr Pots-of-Money we called him!" giggled Laura. "Do you remember how he tipped you into the water so he could get his hands on the map?"

"And he only found the false one and went off on a wild-goose chase," said Nick. "Katie and I have had some great mysteries to solve, but that was the best!"

"I wish I'd known you when you had

your first three adventures," said Laura, sadly. "They sounded marvellous. I don't suppose anything exciting will happen this holidays."

"Well," said Nick, "the milkman told me this morning that a new family is coming to live in that big empty house next door."

"Next door!" exclaimed Laura. "That's been empty for ages. I wonder if Mum knows anything about it."

That evening at supper Laura asked her mother if a family were really coming to live next door.

"Well, I've heard that people are renting the house for the summer," said her mother. "I don't know anything about a family moving in, or whether there are any children."

This was still interesting and the three children looked out for the new family. They arrived two days later but, as they came just as night was falling, it was difficult to see how many there were.

Nick saw them quite by chance. He was half asleep when he heard a car outside. He jumped up and ran to the window to see if it stopped next door – and it did! Out got three or four people, as far as Nick could make out, and one of them seemed fairly small.

"I hope it's a boy!" said Nick to himself as he went back to bed. "I miss having a friend next door like I did when Mum and Dad were alive. Mike was great."

But the boy, if it was a boy, didn't appear at all. The three children watched carefully the next day, but they neither saw nor heard any children.

"You must have been mistaken," said Katie to Nick. "Look, there's the postman coming. Let's see if he knows who's come to live next door."

So they asked him. "I think there's a boy," said the postman. "I had to take a parcel round the back way, and I saw someone in jeans. You'll see him soon enough if there is."

But the boy still didn't appear.

"It's strange," said Nick. "I wonder what he does with himself. He never goes for walks. We never hear him in the garden. I know – let's climb the big chestnut tree and see if we can see him anywhere."

They all three went to the tree. They

climbed up quickly and were soon sitting astride a branch at the top, looking down into their own garden and into the next-door one too.

"Isn't it untidy and overgrown!" said Nick. "I can't see anyone on the lawn, can you?"

"Yes, over there!" said Katie suddenly. The others looked where she pointed, and they saw a small summerhouse. Outside it, in a deckchair, sat a rather fierce-looking woman, knitting. As they watched she put down her knitting, settled herself comfortably, yawned, and seemed to go to sleep.

"No sign of any boy," said Laura. And then all three children stared hard down into the untidy space where the fierce-looking woman sat. Someone was creeping out of the hedge nearby! Someone was on hands and knees, crouching behind the chair!

"A Red Indian!" said Nick, astonished. "Look at those wonderful feathers. What's he going to do?"

The Red Indian suddenly rose to his feet, gave an ear-splitting yell, ran round and round the chair in a very fierce manner, and then disappeared into the hedge again.

The woman woke and sat up angrily. "Kit! I won't have these tricks played on me! I've told you that before. Come and take off those things at once. You always behave so badly when you're playing Indians!"

But Kit didn't appear. The woman went to the hedge and began to poke about with a stick.

"Come out! I shall tell Mr Barton of your behaviour. Your tutor told you not to make any noise at all, and you know perfectly well why. Fancy yelling like that in my ear!" The stick at last found the hiding Kit, and he wriggled out of the hedge, grinning. His face was painted in a very peculiar manner, with bright-coloured stripes across it.

"Sorry, Miss Taylor," he said, "but I'm tired of hanging around here and never doing anything. I'm going to let off steam just for a few minutes and then I'll take these things off and settle down."

And to the watching children's great delight, Kit proceeded to go completely mad, dancing about round the angry Miss Taylor, brandishing what looked like a tomahawk and yelling in a really fearsome manner. He then did a kind of war-dance which was quite amazing, pulled off his wonderful feathered head-dress at the end and bowed gravely to Miss Taylor.

"The show is now ended," he said, and took off the rest of his costume. The children saw that he was a sturdy boy of about thirteen, with laughing eyes, short-cropped hair and a wide grin. He lay down on the grass and began to read, with Miss Taylor grumbling away nearby.

"I think," said Nick, "I rather think we're going to get to know that boy! What a war-dance! I think he might be American, don't you? He spoke with a kind of drawl."

"He's fun, anyway," said Katie. "How can we get to know him? Oh, I know! Let's all dress up in our Red Indian things and squeeze through the hedge tomorrow! We'll pounce on him and give him a terrible fright. That'll be good!"

"Right!" said Nick, sliding down the tree. "We'll do that!"

Chapter 2

THE RED INDIANS HAVE A BAD TIME

The three children were pleased with their plan for introducing themselves to the boy next door.

"It will be just the same kind of surprise he gave to that fierce-looking woman!" said Laura.

Mrs Greyling was astonished to hear there was a boy next door after all. "Well, he's very quiet, I must say," she said. "I wish you three were as quiet! Really, since Uncle Peter's been on his business trip, it's felt like the monkey-house at the zoo, or perhaps the parrot-house. But I'm sure that either of those would be very peaceful compared with our house!"

The next day came. Nick climbed the chestnut tree to see if the boy was anywhere about. At first he couldn't see him, then he heard a cheerful whistling from the summerhouse, and guessed Kit was there.

The fierce-looking woman was nowhere to be seen.

"Good!" said Nick, getting down the tree quickly to tell the others. "The boy's there, but that woman isn't. It would be a good time to jump on Kit now. Come on! Let's get into our things quickly."

They all put on their Red Indian costumes. They looked really fierce, especially after they had painted their faces red, yellow, blue and green.

"How are we going to get into the next-door garden?" asked Laura.

"We'll squeeze through the hedge," said Nick. "It won't be too difficult, though it's pretty thick. Come on!"

They went to the hedge that separated the two gardens. Nick tried to find a way through. At first it seemed impossible, because the hedge was mostly prickly hawthorn.

"We shall tear our things to bits," said Katie. "Oh, no! I've scratched my arm. Nick, we can't get through this hedge, we really can't."

But at last they managed to find a thinner place, and one by one they squeezed through into the next-door garden. It had been neglected for a long time. The paths were lost in weeds and moss. Untrimmed rambler roses hung everywhere, and posts stood crookedly, half dragged down by the weight of the overgrown climbers. There was a very thick copse of trees just before the children reached the lawn where the summerhouse stood, and they hid in the shadow of this.

They lay on their tummies and wriggled along, then crawled as silently as they could through the little wood. It was dark and overgrown in there. One by one the three children crept nearer and nearer to the little enclosed lawn, where they hoped to find Kit.

They didn't see a pair of bright eyes looking in amazement at them from a tree under which they passed. They didn't notice Kit up there, sitting as still as a mouse, watching the three children below crawling by in single file! They didn't hear him slither quietly down the tree when they had passed. He was grinning widely. He guessed that a trick was to be played on him, and he was going to play one, too!

The three children came to the edge of the lawn. The grass had been cut and it was easy to look across to the little summer-house. No one seemed to be there now. What a pity! Perhaps Kit had gone out.

"We'll separate," whispered Nick. "Laura, you go that way. Katie, stay here, and I'll go the other way. Then, when I give a whistle, we'll all dart out of our hiding places and catch Kit when he comes."

So the three separated and, keeping well hidden in the undergrowth around the lawn, they snaked along to surround the grassy patch.

Suddenly Katie had a terrible shock. A fierce face glared at her from out of a bush. It was red and blue all over, and was topped by a magnificent feathered head-dress. It was Kit, of course. He sprang on Katie and before she could shout for help he had jerked her to her feet and set her with her back to a tree.

He whipped a rope from round his waist, and even as Katie yelled in fright he tied her to the tree so that she couldn't escape.

"One prisoner!" said the boy with a grin. "Now for the others!"

Laura was frightened when she heard Katie's yell, and she lay quite still in the undergrowth. But Nick went to his sister's rescue, standing up to see where she was and then rushing towards her.

"Look out, Nick, look out!" yelled Katie as Nick came running up. "That boy is up that tree above us!"

But it was too late! As Nick looked up into the tree, Kit dropped down on him from a branch, and both boys rolled to the ground. Kit was very strong, and it wasn't long before he sat astride Nick and tied up his arms so that he couldn't struggle!

"Another prisoner to tie to a tree!" said Kit with a grin. He shook back the enormous feathers on his head and grinned all over his brilliant red and blue face. "Come on!"

"Come and help me, Laura, quick!" yelled Nick, but Laura was too scared to move. Kit dragged the unwilling Nick to the tree next to Katie and deftly tied him there.

Nick was furious and strained at the rope, trying to free himself. But Kit knew all about knots and loops, and both Katie and Nick were proper prisoners!

And then it was Laura's turn! Kit found her easily because she was frightened. He tied her up to a third tree and then stood in front of them, grinning his wide grin. "Now for a war-dance!" he said.

He did his amazing war-dance again, circling round the trees, yelling and whooping as he went. The three children watched him, angry that they were prisoners, but admiring Kit very much because they thought he was so realistic.

"I suppose you thought you'd creep into my garden and take me prisoner!" said Kit, stopping at last. "You can't trick Christopher Anthony Armstrong like that! I'm going to get my tomahawk and scalp you!"

Kit sped off towards the house. Nick pulled hard at the rope that bound his hands. If only he could free himself and untie the others! But it was no use at all. He couldn't undo the stiff knots.

Then he heard the sound of voices near the house. It seemed as if Kit had met someone. The children listened. Kit was running back without his tomahawk.

"Hey!" he said. "The Dragon's back from her walk! She'll be furious if she sees you here in our garden. I'd better set you free. No, I won't have time! She's coming to the summerhouse. Now listen, stay absolutely still and quiet and maybe she won't see you. I'll go and hide somewhere and try to set you free when she goes back to the house."

Kit disappeared into the bushes. Almost at once the fierce-looking woman appeared, carrying a book. The children's hearts sank as she took a chair from the summerhouse and sat down, opening her book.

They couldn't be seen from where the woman sat, but they all stayed as still as they could. Katie thought the name Kit had for her was very good. She was easily as fierce as a dragon!

And then Laura got a tickle in her throat! She did not dare to clear the tickle away, so she swallowed hard. But the tickle came back, even worse. She swallowed again, and then she coughed! It was a big cough, and it made the woman look up at once.

"Is that you, Kit?" she said. There was

no answer. Poor Laura tried to choke back her next cough, but she couldn't stop it, though Nick frowned fiercely at her. The Dragon got up at once.

She came round a big bush and saw the three children tied to the trees! She stared at them in such amazement that Katie wanted to laugh. It seemed as if the Dragon couldn't believe her eyes!

Nobody said a word. Nick tried to look as if it was the most ordinary thing in the world to be tied to a tree in someone else's garden. And then the Dragon found her voice!

"*What* are you doing here?" she asked. "How dare you come into my garden without permission? Who are you? Why have you tied yourselves up to my trees?"

"We're the children from next door," said Nick. "We came to play with the boy here."

Then the woman said the most extraordinary thing. "Boy?" she said. "A boy here? There's no boy here at all! You must be mad. I shall complain to your mother about you. You are never to come here again. As for there being a boy here, you are quite mistaken. Whoever told you that has been lying. There is no child here."

The children listened to all this, amazed. Nick was about to say that the boy had tied them up, when he caught sight of Kit signalling to him from a bush behind the Dragon's back. It was obvious that Kit did not want Nick to say any more.

The Dragon undid Nick's ropes and Nick set Katie and Laura free. "Now, if I catch you here again," she said, "I shall go straight round to your mother and report you for trespassing."

The children fled home, puzzled and frightened. "It's a mystery," said Nick solemnly when they were safe in their own garden again. "A real mystery. Why should that woman tell such a lie? We've got to find out what it's all about!"

Chapter 3

THE MORNING OF THE ADVENTURE

Nick, Katie and Laura discussed what had happened as they changed their clothes. "We'd better not tell anyone," said Nick. "Perhaps we shouldn't have gone next door without permission. Kit was smart to capture us all. I can't say I liked being tied up like that, but he did come along to set us free when that fierce woman was near."

"I liked him," said Katie. "I wish he'd teach me that war-dance. We'd have to go right down to the bottom of the garden to learn it, though. Aunt Marion would have a fit if we all started yelling so loudly."

"I don't mind meeting that boy again," said Laura, "but I definitely don't want to see that fierce dragon-woman. And why did she say there wasn't a boy there? I suppose she didn't know we'd seen him. She must be crazy if she thought we'd tied ourselves up to the trees!"

"Let's go again tomorrow," said Nick. "Not today, because we've got to go out with Aunt Marion, and anyway, the Dragon might be on the watch. But tomorrow we could."

The two girls were not at all enthusiastic about his suggestion, so Nick decided to go by himself. Before he went, he climbed up the tree to see if the dragon-woman was anywhere about. He couldn't see anyone on the lawn at all. As he slid down the tree to the ground, Laura came running up.

"That fierce woman has just gone out!" she panted. "I went after Russet, he ran out of the front gate, and I saw her going down the lane. Why don't you creep into the next-door garden now, and find Kit?"

"I'm going to," said Nick, and he went to the hedge to find the thin part through which they had all squeezed the day before.

But a great surprise awaited him! It was quite impossible to get through into the next-door garden because somebody had erected strong chain-link fencing all the way down the other side of the hedge!

"Look at that!" said Nick in surprise. "That must have been done yesterday while we were out with Aunt Marion. It's no good squeezing through the hedge now, we couldn't get past that fencing. Why on earth would they do all that to keep us out?"

"It makes me think there really is a mystery next door," said Katie, feeling excited. "We can't get over the top of the fencing either, it's much too high. I think the boy next door is a prisoner."

As the children stood looking through the hedge at the strange, unexpected fence, they heard the sound of distant voices. One was Kit's, and the other was a man's.

"Let's do a bit of shouting to one another," said Nick, "then Kit will know we're playing here, and perhaps come to the hedge to talk to us. We'd better not shout to him. For some reason the people next door obviously don't want us to know Kit lives there. Come on, shout to me and I'll shout back."

So the three began to shout loudly to one another, hoping Kit would hear them and know they were there. But although they waited some time the boy didn't come to the hedge.

"I'll climb the tree again and see if he's

still there," said Nick at last. So he climbed high and looked down into the garden below. Kit was there, but a man was with him this time, not the fierce-looking woman. The man looked stern and rather old, from what Nick could see of him. He appeared to be teaching Kit.

As Nick looked, the man shut the book they were studying, and leaned back in his chair. Nick couldn't hear what he said, but he imagined that he was telling Kit that he was free to amuse himself. Now perhaps the boy would come to talk to them!

But he didn't, for the man still sat there. Kit went into the summerhouse and brought out a ball. He threw it up into the air and caught it. The man bent his head and read his book.

Kit went on and on throwing the ball higher and higher, until suddenly he threw the ball with all his force towards the next-door garden! It curved right over the tree and then disappeared into Nick's own garden, landing with a thud!

"How peculiar!" thought Nick, and watched to see what the boy did next. Kit then produced another ball and began throwing that about, too. Then he sat down, took out his pocket-knife and began to whittle at a stick.

"I'll find his ball," thought Nick, and slid down the tree. "Perhaps he's thrown it over to give us an excuse to take it back to the house and ask for him."

Nick told Katie and Laura what had happened, and they all hunted for the ball, which seemed to have disappeared completely. Everyone looked for it in the most unlikely places. And then Russet found it! He gave a whine and put his paw on it. He rolled it out from under a bush and sat down to receive praise and pats, very sorry to find that it was only a ball that was lost, and not something more interesting!

Nick picked it up. "Good dog!" he said to Russet. "You're worth a hundred cats! Tiger would just sit on a wall and turn her nose up at us if we lost anything."

Laura took it and found that there was a hole in it. She put her fingers inquisitively inside and was just about to take them out again when her eyes widened in excitement.

"What's up?" said Nick.

"There's something in here," said Laura. "Wait, let me get it out!"

She wriggled her finger and thumb about inside the old ball, and heard the crackle of paper. She got hold of it at last and pulled it out.

"It's a note!" she said. "What a brilliant

way of sending us a message!"

"Right under the nose of that man, too," said Nick. "I think that Kit is very smart. What does it say?"

Laura unfolded the note. It was quite short, and written in strong, bold handwriting.

TO MY THREE PRISONERS

Don't believe the Dragon when she says I'm not here! She has a Reason. I'm very lonely and bored, and I should like to know you. But you mustn't be seen here. They've put a chain-link fence all round the garden now to keep you out. But holes can be dug underneath! What about it? Chuck this ball back with an answer when you get a chance!

K.A

This was really exciting! The three children stared at one another in astonishment. There was definitely a mystery, and only Kit could explain it. They must get into the garden next door again somehow. But they would have to be very careful not to be caught.

They all read the note again. It seemed

even stranger and more thrilling the second time.

"We'll write an answer," said Nick. "And of course we'll dig a hole underneath a bit of fencing and get through that way. It's a brilliant idea. But we'd better do it at the bottom of the garden in case anyone sees us."

"We'll have to take turns at it," said Katie. "We'll have to keep guard. Oh, it will be great! When we get into the next-door garden again, we'll have to keep a lookout for the Dragon. It makes me shiver to think of it!"

"Shall we answer the note?" asked Laura. "What shall we say?"

They went indoors to get paper and pencil, and Katie wrote an answer.

TO OUR CAPTOR

We're going to dig a hole. Can you get out at night? It would be best to meet then. Say, tonight at midnight, by the summer-house, if possible. Send the ball back with an answer.

NICK, LAURA AND KATIE

Nick threw the ball back, because he

could throw the farthest. Katie sat at the top of the chestnut tree to watch where it fell. She came down giggling so much that the other two couldn't get a word out of her for some time.

"The ball fell right on that man's book!" giggled Katie. "It gave him such a fright! And then he turned round and began to blame Kit for throwing it at him. Kit just picked up the ball and went into the summerhouse with it."

"That must have been funny!" said Nick, with a chuckle. "I expect Kit's read the note by now. Come on, let's see where would be the best place to dig a hole. We could start that now. Where's Russet? He can come, too, and scrape with his paws. He'd be quite a help."

So all three went off down the garden, carrying spades. Russet followed behind, hoping he wouldn't be sent away.

They examined the hedge thoroughly, and found the place to dig the hole.

"Between these two hawthorn trees would be best," said Nick. "We can cut away the lower branches so that they won't scratch us while we work. We can dig deep down here because the ground is soft. I guess it'll take us tome time to burrow right under the fencing the other side."

"Well, we don't need a very big hole," said Katie. "We can wriggle down the passage like Red Indians do. It'll be good fun! Russet, you go and begin the hole just there, look!"

So Russet obligingly went down between the hawthorn trees and began to scrape so violently that the earth flew up in the children's faces.

"Laura, you keep guard," said Nick. "Katie, you and I will start digging. Come on. Get away now, Russet. You've made a great beginning!"

So the hole was begun, and the three children worked hard to make it big enough to wriggle down that night. It was very exciting! They planned to go through the hole at midnight! They were all longing for twelve o'clock to come.

Chapter 4

THE HOLE UNDER THE FENCE

The children worked flat out at digging the hole under the chain-link fencing. When Mrs Greyling called them in to their lunch they were tired and hungry, and also extremely dirty.

"Good heavens!" she said. "What in the world have you been doing with yourselves? You look as if you've been trying to dig down to Australia!"

"Well, we have been digging," said Laura. The others frowned at her. They thought Laura was silly even to hint at their secret.

"Whatever for?" asked Mrs Greyling. "I can't believe you've been gardening!"

But to her surprise nobody seemed very keen to talk about it.

"It's a sort of secret," said Nick at last. Aunt Marion was very understanding about secrets. She nodded her head.

"I see," she said. "Well, you keep your secret! I won't pry into it."

Everyone heaved a sigh of relief. They ate their lunch hungrily, and then went out again to go on with their work. They talked about Kit in low voices as they dug.

"He must be dreadfully bored living in that house with the dragon-woman and that stern-looking man," said Nick. "Nobody to play with or have a laugh with."

"And people saying he isn't there at all!" said Katie. "What a storyteller that woman is!"

"Shh!" said Laura suddenly. She was on guard, watching to see if anyone came down their garden or the next. "Someone's coming down next-door's garden!"

At once the children hid their spades under a bush and crouched down low in some tall grass nearby. They heard the sound of someone brushing against the overgrown bushes next door, and then came the sound of voices.

"This garden is very thick and overgrown. No one can see into it from the outside. That's good!"

"Have you been all round?" came the

voice of the dragon-woman. Nick tried to see who her companion was. He felt sure it was the stern-looking man.

"Yes. I went when George put up the wire-fencing," said the other voice. "No one can get in now, and no one can see in."

The two people came near to where the children had been working. Russet growled softly. Laura put her hand on his collar to keep him quiet. All the children shivered with excitement, fearing that their digging might be discovered.

But luckily it wasn't. The two people went slowly by, and neither of them saw the deep hole under the fencing. When they had gone out of sight and hearing, the diggers began again. This time Nick was on guard.

By the time tea was ready, the hole was almost big enough to wriggle through.

"We can easily finish after tea," said Nick. "Ow, my back aches! O-o-oh! I don't like standing up straight at all!"

"We'd better clean ourselves up a bit before Aunt Marion sees us," said Katie, looking at their dirty clothes and hands. So they all washed carefully and brushed their clothes well. They ate such an enormous tea that Mrs Greyling was really surprised.

"Anyone would think you had all been very hard at work, the way you're eating," she said, as plate after plate was emptied. "Nick, I can't believe you want another bun. That must be the fourth you've eaten!"

"Wrong, Aunt Marion," said Nick. "It's the fifth!"

The hole was finished by six o'clock. It was like a curving trench that sloped downwards to the fencing, underneath it, and then up the other side. It was quite big enough to wriggle through. It had been very difficult to do the other side, but somehow Nick had managed to scramble through underneath and dig the trench widely there, too.

"Now, we'll all wriggle through on our tummies," said Nick, and one by one they struggled to get under the fencing and into the next-door garden.

It was really exciting. Russet was delighted too and ran down the trench and back, his tail wagging nineteen to the dozen!

"Don't you think we'd better cover up

the hole this side with branches, or something?" said Katie, when they all stood among the overgrown grass and bushes in the next-door garden. "It can so easily be seen now."

"Yes, we'll do that," said Nick and began to break some branches to spread over the trench. "We'll drag these across the entrance when we go back. The last one can do it."

Russet suddenly stood still, his ears up, his nose twitching and his tail quivering. He had heard something. He gave a little growl.

"Somebody's coming!" said Laura, in a whisper. "Come on back."

But there was no time to get back. The stern-looking man was taking an evening walk around the grounds, and the children caught sight of him between the trees.

"Climb a tree, quick!" whispered Nick. "Go on, Laura, I'll give you a leg up!"

He pushed poor Laura up a tree, and then swung himself up, too. Katie had already climbed into one. The man came nearer. Luckily he was walking very slowly.

"What about Russet?" whispered Laura.

"He can't climb a tree! Lie down, Russet. Lie down!"

But Russet didn't. He stood under Laura's tree, looking up at her and Nick in great surprise. "He'll give us away!" said Laura.

But as soon as the man came near, Russet left the tree and ran up to him, his teeth bared, growling fiercely. The man stopped in astonishment.

"Well! How did you get in here?" he cried. "I shouldn't have thought there was any way through this fencing! You must have been here yesterday when we fenced in the grounds and you couldn't get out. Well, out you go now and stop that silly growling or you'll be sorry!"

Russet didn't like the man's voice. His tail dropped. He let the man take hold of his collar and lead him sternly off up the garden towards the house.

"He's going to let him out of the garden gate," whispered Laura to Nick.

"We'd better wait here a little while in case the man comes back too quickly for us to get through the tunnel," said Nick.

So they waited in silence, wishing that

Kit would come along. But he didn't.

Suddenly they heard a pitter-patter of feet and a swishing of bushes as some little body came up to their trees.

"It's Russet again!" said Laura with a giggle. "The man let him out and he went down the garden, found our hole, and came through it to fetch us! Isn't he clever? I hope the man doesn't come walking back again, because if he does he'll be very surprised to see Russet here!"

"You'd better shin down the tree and get back through the hole with Russet," said Nick. "Then keep a watch out and give a whistle when you're sure it's safe for Katie and me to come down."

So Laura slid down the tree and went to the trench with Russet licking her ankles in delight. She wriggled down on her tummy, slid through the hole and up the other side. It was not good for her clothes. She made up her mind to wear her very oldest things the next time!

When she got to the other side, she stood up and cautiously went up and down the hedge to see if anyone was in the next garden. But it seemed quite safe. So she gave a whistle, and Nick and Katie slid down their trees and were soon wriggling through the hole. Nick went last and pulled the broken branches over the trench. It was quite well hidden then.

"This is very exciting, isn't it?" he said, as he tried to brush the dirt off himself. "Aren't we filthy? Aunt Marion will want to know a bit more about our secret if we keep on going in as filthy as this. We'd better look out some raggedy old things to wear for this tunnelling business!"

Mrs Greyling was not pleased when they appeared for supper, although they had made themselves as clean as possible. She sent them to have a bath as soon as they appeared.

"This digging secret, whatever it is, has got to stop," she said. "You are ruining your clothes."

"All right, Aunt Marion, we won't dig any more," promised Nick, and went off to have a bath.

The children ate an enormous supper, but when they had finished they couldn't stop yawning. For once they didn't argue about going to bed early. "We want to be awake at midnight, so we might as well get a bit of sleep first," said Nick to the others, when they were alone.

"How will we wake up?" asked Laura.

"I'll set my alarm for a quarter to twelve, and wake you both then," said Nick. "Come on, let's go to bed. I'm tired!"

So they all went to bed and, as soon as their heads were on their pillows, they fell asleep. At last Nick's alarm went off under his pillow. He had put the little clock there, afraid that it might wake up Aunt Marion if he stood it on a table. It woke him with a jump and he groped under the pillow to turn it off.

Then he went to wake the two girls. They sat up in bed, excited.

"Put on those old things we got ready after supper," whispered Nick. "Don't be long! It's a quarter to midnight!"

Within five minutes, the three children and Russet were creeping quietly out of the house, Nick's torch lighting the way. They went down the dark garden to the hole under the fence. What was going to happen in the next-door garden after midnight?

Chapter 5

THROUGH THE HOLE AT MIDNIGHT

The three children made their way down beside the hedge that separated the two gardens. Russet ran with them, astonished and excited. Could this be a rabbit-hunt in the middle of the night?

Two great gleaming eyes of green suddenly appeared in the light of the torch. Laura gave a little scream of fright. Russet stopped, then gave a glad yelp and rushed forward. The eyes disappeared, and there came the noise of something bounding up a tree.

"It was only Tiger," said Katie, relieved. "How weird her eyes looked, gleaming out of the darkness like that! Laura, get Russet back before he starts to bark."

Russet was hauled away from the tree in which Tiger sat, her eyes gleaming green again. The little company went on down the garden. Laura felt a little shaky at the knees but she was determined not to let it show.

They came to the hole under the fencing. Nick shone his torch on it. "You go first," he said to Katie. "Then Laura. I'll stand here and shine the torch so you can see, then I'll follow on."

One by one they wriggled through the hole, until they were all standing safely on the other side with Russet at their heels, his tail wagging with pleasure. Nick shone his torch on the thick undergrowth.

"I hope the light of my torch won't be seen," he whispered. "I'll keep my hand over it as much as I can. Let's all hold hands and try and walk in single file."

So they did that, and stumbled through the long grass and round thick bushes until they came to the little wooded part that surrounded the lawn.

"Now, whereabouts is the summer-house?" said Nick in a whisper. "Look, what's that?"

They all stared at a red glow a little way off. It disappeared. Then it came again, then it vanished once more.

"It's the light of a red-bulbed torch being

turned on and off," whispered Katie. "I bet it's Kit in the summerhouse." The light glowed red again, then vanished.

"Kit! Is it you?" whispered Nick.

A low voice answered him: "Yes. Gee, you're punctual! It's only just striking twelve. Listen!"

A clock could be heard striking from the house. The children crowded inside the summerhouse with Russet at their heels, his tail banging against their legs as he wagged it.

"Are we safe here?" asked Nick, feeling for the seat that ran round the little summerhouse. "What's that you've got? A special torch?"

"Yeah," said Kit, and he switched on the dim red glow again. "I thought it would be a signal to show you where to come. We're quite safe here now. I heard my tutor snoring away in bed, and I know the Dragon won't guess I'm out, because I left a bolster down the middle of my bed in case she looked into my room."

"Clever," said Katie. "Kit, that was a smart idea of yours to send us a message inside your old ball. We dug a hole under

45

the fencing, just as you suggested."

"Good for you!" said Kit. "I thought you'd manage to do it. I'm glad you're next door. I guess I'll have a bit of fun sometimes now."

"Kit, why did the Dragon say there was no boy here?" Nick asked curiously. "It was an absolute lie."

"Sure. But there's a reason for it," said Kit. "If I tell you, will you promise faithfully not to tell a single soul?"

"Of course," said all three at once.

"Well, here goes," said Kit solemnly. He switched on the red glow again, and his face shone oddly in the crimson light. "There's somebody after my life!"

Nobody said anything for a minute. They were all too stunned.

"What do you mean, Kit?" asked Nick at last.

"It's like this," said Kit. "I'm American, and I'm very rich. My grandfather left an enormous fortune to my father, and when he disappeared and was presumed to have been killed in an aeroplane crash, the money came to me."

"Oh, did your father die when the plane

crashed, then?" said Nick, feeling sorry for Kit.

"The plane was completely burned," said Kit. "Nobody could be rescued from it. My father was known to be travelling in it, so he must have lost his life when it crashed and burned out. Anyway, I inherited his fortune."

"But I don't see why anyone should be after your life just because you're rich," said Laura, puzzled.

"Ah, but if I die, there's a horrible uncle of mine who will inherit my money," said Kit. "It's an uncle I've never seen. He's tried to kidnap me twice already. I guess I wouldn't have much of a chance if he did get hold of me!"

This all sounded most extraordinary to the three children. They looked at Kit's earnest face glowing in the red light.

"Oh, that's why you're in hiding, then," said Laura. "Because you *are* in hiding, aren't you? Is the Dragon looking after you, and your tutor? What is a tutor, by the way?"

"Oh, a teacher," said Kit. "They found this lonely house in this desolate bit of country – sorry, I know it's lovely with its rivers and hills, but it's pretty dull when you're used to living in towns. Anyway, they found this house and rented it to hide me in, until they can track down my wicked uncle and stop him coming after me. We travelled over from America and gave him the slip."

"Will he come to this country and look for you?" asked Katie, a little shiver going down her back.

"Sure he will!" said Kit. "But don't you worry! I'm not afraid. The only thing I'm afraid of is being bored and lonely. I guess if the Dragon had known there were three children in your house she'd never have come here! But she heard there was one little girl and that was all."

"That's all there used to be," said Laura. "That was me, but now Katie and Nick live here too."

"I'm sorry about your father," said Nick. "Both our parents died in a car crash nearly two years ago. It must be dreadful for you, all on your own with just the Dragon and a tutor."

"Yeah, it's been pretty bad at times, but

now we're gonna have some fun," said Kit. "Like me to teach you that war-dance? It was taught to me by a real live native American. And my Red Indian suit is a real one too, not a toy one like yours."

Kit sounded very exciting. The three children thought he would be a marvellous friend to have.

"Nick will enjoy having you next door," said Katie. "Sometimes he gets fed up with only Laura and me to do things with. We go to school in a town eight miles away and our friends are scattered all over the place. Faldham is a very small village and there are no boys of Nick's age living here."

"We'll all have a great time together!" said Kit. "I haven't got any sisters, and I've always wished that I had."

"Is that dragon-woman very fierce?" asked Katie. "Who is she?"

"Oh, she's not bad," said Kit. "My tutor, Mr Barton, got her to keep an eye on me, and to watch out that nobody came near me, or knew about me here. I'm not supposed to leave this garden at all, or show myself. If I obey her, she's all right, but I honestly believe she'd get a stick and beat me if I didn't do what she said!"

"I shouldn't be surprised if she did, either," said Katie. "She looks like that. I hope she never discovers us here!"

"Do you think you really are safe here?" asked Laura anxiously. "It would be so awful if your wicked uncle discovered you and tried to kidnap you again."

"I don't see how he possibly can," said Kit. "Anyway, I'm not afraid! But please don't tell my secret to anyone at all, will you?"

The others all shook their heads.

"Good," said Kit. "Now, let's make plans. I don't see why I shouldn't sometimes get through that tunnel of yours and come into your garden, if I can be sure that no one will spot me."

"I know what we can do. Why don't you come out boating with us on the river one day?" said Nick eagerly. "We know a secret way down there so you'll be quite safe. We've a boat of our own, and we can have fun. We could take our lunch out sometimes and picnic on a little island we know, and swim there. That'd be good, wouldn't it?"

"You bet!" said Kit, and his eyes shone in the red light. "I'll have to think of some way to outwit the Dragon, though. It would have to be on a day when she goes out and leaves me safely penned up here in the grounds. We'd better wait a few days till she's settled down here. You can come in to see me, can't you? There's a big attic at the top of the house that Mr Barton has given me to play in. We could go there. I can lock the door so that no one can come in."

"Oh, yes," said Nick. "And we could play all sorts of games in your grounds, too, because they're so thick and overgrown."

"Listen, you come along again tomorrow," said Kit. "After lunch, okay?"

"All right," said Nick. "Hey, this is going to be fun, isn't it? Sort of secret and exciting. I hope that wicked uncle of yours doesn't find out where you are. It would be annoying if you had to go and hide somewhere else just as we had got to know you!"

"We'll come tomorrow, then," said Laura, "and we'll bring our Red Indian things. You can teach us that war-dance."

"We'd better go now," said Nick, getting

up. "See you tomorrow. Come on, girls. We'll skirt round the edge of the lawn before I put on my torch. Goodnight, Kit."

"Goodnight, and thanks for coming," said the American boy in his nice drawly voice. "I'll be right at the very bottom of our grounds, waiting for you. Bye!"

The three children went out of the little summerhouse, with Russet at their heels. They found their way by the light of Nick's little torch to the hole under the fence. They wriggled through and then made their way up to their own house.

"Goodnight!" whispered Nick at his bedroom door. "Now, keep your mouths shut about all this – especially you, Laura!"

"I shan't say a word, I promise," whispered Laura. The girls slipped into their bedroom and snuggled into bed.

"It's going to be exciting!" said Katie.

But she couldn't have guessed just how exciting it was all going to be!

Chapter 6

An Exciting Climb

The next day the children got out their Red Indian things ready to go into the next-door garden and play with Kit.

"I'm longing to learn that whooping war-dance," said Laura. "But won't we spoil our Red Indian things when we wriggle through the hole?"

"Yes, we will," said Nick. "What shall we do?"

"Easy!" said Katie. "Put them in a sack, tie up the neck of the sack with a long bit of string, and then drag it through after us!"

"Good idea!" said Nick. Katie went off to find a sack, and soon came back with one from the garden shed.

They stuffed their Red Indian things inside it. Then, with their very oldest clothes on, they set off down the garden with Russet at their heels.

Mrs Greyling called after them: "Now

don't do any more of that dirty digging, please!"

"No, we've finished that," called back Nick.

"Take some plums from the tree to eat at eleven o'clock!" called Mrs Greyling again. So the children went to the plum tree and stuffed their pockets full of ripe plums. They took enough for Kit too.

They came to the hole. It was still there, hidden by branches. "Good!" said Nick. "Come on. You go first, Katie, then Laura."

Nick pulled the sack of clothes after him, and it slid through the tunnel, much to Russet's amazement. He pranced after it, trying to snap at it.

Soon the three of them were standing cautiously on the other side of the tunnel, brushing the dirt off their clothes, listening for the sound of someone coming. But there was no sound to be heard except the wind in the trees and a chaffinch calling somewhere.

"It's a good thing Russet is such a quiet sort of dog," said Katie to Laura. "If he was a barking dog, we couldn't possibly take him with us."

"I wonder where Kit is," said Nick. "Let's find him before we change into our Red Indian things. Oh, no, it's going to rain!"

The children stared through the trees in dismay. The sky had clouded over and looked very low and black. Big drops of rain fell on their upturned faces.

"Come on, let's go down to the bottom of the garden," said Nick at last. "We'd better find Kit and see if there's any shelter."

They made their way down the overgrown garden.

"Hi!" said a voice from up a tree. Kit seemed to love being up trees! "Glad you've come, I've been waiting ages for you."

"Hi!" said Laura. "I hope this rain stops soon."

It was now pouring down and the children were getting very wet. They stood under the trees, hoping the clouds would blow over.

"There's nowhere we can shelter except the summerhouse, and I daren't take you there in case the Dragon comes to find me," Kit said gloomily.

"What about that big playroom you said

you've got?" asked Nick. "Could we get there without being seen?"

"Yeah, there might be a way," said Kit, after thinking for a minute. "Are you good at climbing?"

"Yes," said Nick. "Quite good."

"Listen," said Kit, his eyes beginning to shine. "If we went right round the garden to the other side, we could creep almost up to the house without being seen, because the trees are so thick there. There's an enormous ash tree that reaches right up to the top of the house, and its branches touch the walls. We couldn't climb up the trunk; it's too tall. But we could get on to the flat garage roof, then into the branches and up. I guess we could easily get through the attic window then."

"Right, let's try," said Katie. "It sounds fine if only nobody sees us!"

"There are no windows that side of the house where the garage is, except for the two attic windows at the top," said Kit, thinking. "It ought to be all right. I'll tell you what I'll do. I'll go to the house and make sure that no one's about. Then, when you hear me whistle a tune, climb up on to the garage roof and into the tree."

"I'll go first," said Nick. "I don't want the girls to try anything dangerous."

"Sure!" said Kit. "What about the dog? He can't climb."

They all stood and wondered what to do with the little spaniel. Russet looked up at them inquiringly. He didn't want to be left out of anything.

"Couldn't you bundle him into the sack of clothes?" asked Kit. "Would he stay there without making a noise? I could carry him upstairs with me then, hidden in the sack."

"I don't expect he'd mind a bit," said Laura. "He's used to all kinds of strange games, aren't you, Russet?"

"Woof," answered Russet politely, his ears quivering.

"Let's try him now," said Nick. So they stuffed Russet into the bag of clothes, and then Nick put the sack over his shoulder. Russet gave a muffled yelp and tried to wriggle, but when Laura patted the sack and said, "It's all right, Russet. Good dog, it's all right!" he settled down without a fuss.

"Okay. We can take him up to the attic like that," said Kit. "Now, come on! I'll take you to the back of the garage, and show you what to do. Then I'll go in and scout round to make sure everything's safe."

Kit took them round the bottom of the grounds. The rain poured down and everyone was very wet and uncomfortable. They crept quietly up the other side of the big garden and at last, through a thicket of trees and bushes, they came to the back of the big garage, which was built on to the side of the house.

The children looked up at it. "How do we get up there, to begin with?" asked Nick. "We can't fly!"

"I'll get a ladder," said Kit. "There's one in the garage."

He disappeared, and came out a minute or two later carrying a light ladder. He set it against the wall of the garage and it just reached the top.

"Right, up we go!" he said. He set the sack on the ground and let Russet out for a minute to get some air. "We can put him back again when I'm ready to go indoors," he added. He went up the ladder, climbed out on to the flat roof and hauled Nick up too.

"Now, you can easily get into the ash tree branches from here," said Kit, pointing to where the enormous tree spread out strong branches over the garage roof. "Once you're in the tree you can climb from branch to branch till you reach the attic window. It's that one on the left, okay? I'll slip indoors now and go up to the attic with the sack of clothes and Russet. Wait till you hear me whistle before you do anything."

The two boys climbed down again and Russet was popped into the sack once more. He was rather astonished, but made no fuss. Kit put him over his shoulder, winked merrily at Nick, and disappeared round the garage to go into the house.

Before two minutes had passed they heard the sound of "Yankee Doodle" being whistled loudly from above. They looked up and saw Kit at the attic window, which he had opened widely. He nodded and grinned at them.

"Come on," said Nick in excitement. "I'll go up first and give you a hand."

He went up the ladder and climbed on to the flat garage roof. Laura came next, then Katie. Nick looked at the ash tree and chose a sturdy branch that stuck out over the roof. "This looks a nice easy one to climb," he said. "Laura, do you think you can manage all right?"

"Yes, of course I can!" said Laura. "I'm not as quick as you two, but I can climb perfectly well!"

The three children soon reached the branch that was level with the attic window and slid along it to the sill.

But how were they to get on to the sill? The branch dipped under their weight when they went towards the end of it. Kit

watched, his eyes wrinkling up as he wondered how to help.

"Wait a minute!" he said. He disappeared and came back with a broad plank he had taken from the box-room. He pushed it out of the window and Nick caught the end when it came to him. "Tie it firmly to the branch with this rope, then it won't slip," said Kit, and he threw a coil of strong rope to Nick, who bound the plank tightly to the tree. One end rested firmly on a broad branch, the other on the sill of the attic window. Now they could slide carefully along the plank from the tree to the window.

"Brilliant!" said Kit, as one by one the three came in at the window. "We can always come in this way without being seen if we want to. We'll leave the plank tied there. No one is likely to spot it!"

They stood in the big attic and looked round. It had slanting ceilings, and a skylight set in the middle. Boxes and trunks were piled in one corner. Here and there were books and games belonging to Kit, an electric railway set, a carpentry bench and tools, a half-made model schooner, and various old toys.

"Now, let's dress up in our things and you can teach us that war-dance," said Nick. "Come on! Are you sure that dragon-woman isn't anywhere about, or your tutor?"

"No, they're both out – isn't it lucky?" said Kit. "We can make what noise we like! Hurry up and we'll get going."

They all changed into their Red Indian things. "We'd better lock the door, hadn't we?" said Katie, feeling that she didn't want anyone to burst suddenly in on them.

"Sure," said Kit, and he locked it. Then he began to teach them to dance. How they yelled, how they whooped, how they stamped round in a circle, all dressed up in their Red Indian costumes and feathers! They enjoyed themselves thoroughly.

And then they got a dreadful shock! Someone began banging on the door; someone tried to turn the door handle. A voice called out sternly: "Kit, what are you doing? What's all this noise? Unlock the door at once!"

"It's my tutor back!" said Kit. "Oh, no! What are we going to do?"

Chapter 7

Mr Barton is Angry

The four children and Russet stared at one another in dismay. Russet gave a little growl, but Laura stopped him at once.

"You mustn't be discovered here," said Kit in a whisper. "Where can I hide you?"

"Open the door, Kit, open it at once!" cried the voice of Kit's stern tutor. The children knew there was no time to escape out of the window. They looked round in despair. Nick caught sight of two or three big trunks and ran to them, beckoning to Katie and Laura. Maybe they could hide in them!

"All right, Mr Barton, I'll open the door," said Kit. "I was only practising my Indian war-dance."

He whispered into Nick's ear. "You try and get into the trunks while I pretend to fumble with the key in the door. That will give you a little time!"

Nick nodded and opened the lid of a big old trunk. He pushed Laura inside and shut the lid while Katie climbed into another trunk. Then he jumped into a large box and crouched down inside it. He pulled the lid over him.

Meanwhile Kit had gone to the door and was rattling the handle and jiggling the key as if he were trying his hardest to open it. His tutor was calling out impatiently all the time.

"Kit! What are you doing? Can't you open this door?"

"I'm trying my hardest!" panted Kit. "Just be patient, Mr Barton. I think the key is turning."

He turned it and the door opened. His tutor came in, looking very angry. He gazed round the room as if he expected to find it full of children. But there was no one there except Kit, who looked remarkably innocent.

"Do you mean to tell me that it was only you making all that dreadful noise?" cried his tutor disbelievingly. "I know that you often make a noise that sounds like a whole menagerie, but it's impossible to believe that all those yells and shoutings and stamps were made by one boy!"

Then an awful thing happened! Everyone had forgotten about Russet! The little spaniel had run into a corner in fright when the banging at the door had become really loud, but now he came out to see what the matter was, and stood by Kit, wagging his tail a little. Kit was afraid he might go and sniff at one of the trunks in which the others had hidden, and he picked him up at once. His tutor stared at the dog in the greatest amazement.

"That dog again!" he said. "How did he get up here? Did you bring him? And where in the world did he come from? There's fencing all round the garden!"

"I brought him up here," said Kit truthfully. "I found him in the garden. I'm so lonely, you see, and I do like him."

"He must belong to the people next door," said Mr Barton. "I wish I knew how he gets into the garden."

"Maybe he comes through a rabbit hole," suggested Kit. "He's quite a little dog, not much more than a puppy."

"Woof!" said Russet, hearing the word

"rabbit" with great pleasure.

"He must go back," said Kit's tutor firmly. "Well, I would never have believed that you and a small dog could make such a terrible noise together. Kindly do not lock the door again, Kit."

"Shall I take the dog back?" asked Kit.

"Of course not," said his tutor. "You know we don't want you to be seen at all. And I especially don't want those children next door to know you are here. They'd tell everyone about you, and then the secret would be out!" He picked up Russet and went out of the door.

"I'm going to take this dog back now," he said. "I want to give you some lessons when I return, so get your books and take them down to my study. Be ready for me."

"Yes, sir," said Kit dolefully. As soon as his tutor was out of the room he flew to the big box in which Nick was hidden. "You must come out at once!" he hissed.

Nick was just about to push up the lid when to Kit's horror his tutor came back again to tell him something he had forgotten. The boy sat down at once on the lid of the box to prevent Nick from opening it and popping his head up!

Nick did not know that Mr Barton was back, and he couldn't think why the box lid wouldn't open. He pushed hard at it and began to speak to Kit.

Kit sat hard on the box, drumming his heels against it and whistling to hide the sound of Nick's voice.

His tutor was annoyed with him. "Kit! Don't drum your heels like that and whistle while I'm talking to you! Get up at once!"

Kit had to get up, but luckily by that time Nick had guessed something was up, and was quiet again. The three children were all trembling with excitement.

"I came back to tell you to get out the big world globe," said Kit's tutor. "You know where it is. Put it in the study ready for us. Don't be long, Kit, because I shall be back in a minute. And change your clothes."

He disappeared again and Kit waited until he heard him going down the stairs. Then he quickly shut and locked the attic door and ran to the trunks. He pulled out Katie and Laura, and Nick jumped out of his box, too.

"That was a narrow escape!" said Nick. "We'd better leave at once. Come on, girls, along the plank and down the tree we go! When will we see you again, Kit?"

"Don't know," said Kit dismally. "It's still pouring with rain. No good doing anything out of doors today, and I daren't risk you coming back to the attic. What about tomorrow?"

"We were planning to go down the river," said Nick eagerly. "There's a big bend of it we haven't properly explored that's just beyond the tiny island we know. Like to come with us? Can you escape for a few hours, do you think? You could wriggle through our hole."

"I'll come somehow!" promised Kit. "I'll get the Dragon to let me have a picnic lunch by myself at the bottom of the garden, but I'll bring my lunch through the hole and join you. What time? Twelve o'clock?"

"Yes, that would be fine," said Nick, going to the window. "Come on, girls. Kit's tutor will be back if we don't hurry!"

They got on to the plank one by one and slid cautiously along it to the tree. Then down they climbed and jumped on to the flat roof of the garage. Down the ladder and on to the ground, then right round the garden and through the hole. The rain had made it muddy, and their lovely Red Indian suits were in a fine mess by the time they reached the other side.

"Never mind, we'll wait till they're dry and then brush them well," said Katie. "I wonder where Russet is?"

They soon knew, for he came rushing to meet them when they went back to the house. Mrs Greyling had been surprised when Mr Barton had brought him back. She had thought he was with the children.

"Aunt Marion, can we go for a picnic down to the river tomorrow?" asked Nick. "It would be fun. If it's fine we might swim too."

"Yes, you can go," said Aunt Marion. "I'll get a picnic lunch ready for you."

So the next day the three children and Russet went to the bottom of the garden to see if Kit would be able to keep his word and come with them. It was not quite twelve o'clock. The sun shone down warmly out of a blue sky. The rain had all gone and it was a blazing August day.

They waited for Kit. Twelve o'clock came, but no Kit. The children waited a little longer. Russet suddenly ran down the hole and disappeared. He didn't come back when Laura whistled to him, which was very naughty.

"Smelled a rabbit, I suppose," said Laura in disgust. "Well, I only hope Kit's tutor doesn't catch him again."

"It's a quarter past twelve," said Nick, looking at his watch. "We'll wait for Russet to come back then we'd better not wait for Kit any more. It's a shame. He would have enjoyed a picnic on the river."

"Here's Russet!" said Laura, after five minutes had gone by. "Naughty dog! Where have you been?"

"Look, Laura, he's got something tied to his collar!" said Katie suddenly. "It's a note, I think."

"So it is!" said Laura, and she undid the screwed-up note. She unfolded it and read it out to the others.

Can you possibly wait for me? Mr Barton has made me do extra work as I asked for the

*afternoon off for a picnic in the garden. I shall
be free at half past twelve and can come then,
with my food. Do wait!*

K.A.

"Good old Russet!" said Nick, patting
the dog. "You didn't go after rabbits then!
You went and found Kit and he managed to
give you a message for us! It's nearly half
past twelve, so there's not long to wait."

They waited patiently, and just after the
half hour they heard a loud whistling.
"Kit!" said Nick, and he stood up to show
the boy the hole.

Kit wriggled through it on his tummy,
and grinned as he stood up in the children's
garden. "A pretty good way in and out, if a
bit dirty," he said. "Thanks for waiting. Mr
Barton said I could have the afternoon off if
I did extra lessons this morning. I hope
nobody goes hunting for me this afternoon!
Come on. Which way is it? Hey, I feel just
like an escaped prisoner – I *am* going to
enjoy myself!"

Kit was a wonderful companion. He told
jokes and knew stories that made everyone
fall about laughing until they begged him

to stop. Nick, Katie and Laura were very happy to have him with them. They let themselves out of the gate at the bottom of their garden and went across the fields, carrying their food in rucksacks.

"We've got a boat of our own on the river," said Nick. "We thought we'd take it out today and row to the little island we know, have our lunch there and then do a bit of exploring beyond."

"You never know when I might want a good hiding place!" said Kit with a laugh. "We could pretend that we're looking for one where nobody could find me even if they hunted for weeks!"

"Oh yes, that would be fun!" said Katie. "Look, there's our boat! Come on, let's hurry and push her off. I'm longing to be on the river!"

They got into the boat, carefully stowing their lunches where Russet couldn't get them. Nick rowed and they all sang as they went up river. What fun they were going to have!

Chapter 8

THE HOUSEBOAT ON THE RIVER

"You'll like our tiny island," said Laura. "One year a swan nested there. And there are heaps of kingfishers, too. There's a little sandy beach where we can swim and lie in the sun afterwards."

"Great!" said Kit. "It sounds pretty good to me! Let me take the oars now, Nick."

Kit rowed very strongly and the little boat shot quickly along over the water. After a while they came to a bend and then the river widened out. Tucked away in the bend was a tiny island.

"That's our island," said Nick. "It's nothing but a mound on which grow a few trees, some blackberry bushes and grass. But it's fun. There are no rabbits though, Russet!"

"Woof!" said Russet gloomily. He was sitting at the prow of the boat, watching the water as if he meant to jump into it at any moment. Laura had her hand on his collar just in case he really did!

The children ran the boat on to the sandy beach. They jumped out and hauled it up a little way. Then they went over the tiny island. It was so small that it took only a few minutes to walk all the way round it!

"It's wonderful," said Kit. "I wish it was mine. Now, what about lunch, or shall we swim first?"

"Let's swim," said Nick. "I'm boiling!"

They had their swimsuits on under their clothes, so in no time they were all diving into the water.

It was very hot in the sun. The four children and Russet lay on the sun-baked beach and let themselves dry. Then they had their lunch.

They were terribly hungry. Kit had not got such a nice lunch as the others, so they shared with him. Russet had some biscuits and one ham sandwich which Laura spared him out of her share. After lunch they felt lazy and sleepy.

"But don't let's go to sleep!" said Kit, sitting up. "I haven't come out to sleep! I want to explore. I don't know what your countryside is really like, you know. It's quite different from the States. Let's take the boat and go and explore the bit you said you didn't know. Round the bend where the water is so blue and where those cute little birds are swimming, bobbing their heads like clockwork!"

"Moorhens!" said Nick with a laugh. "Come on, then. Into the boat!"

They all got into the boat and Russet took his place at the prow. The boys took an oar each and rowed off round the big bend of the river. The banks were thickly lined with trees and the water was very deep.

"It's lovely here," said Laura, lying back and letting one hand drag in the water as they went along. "I could go on like this for miles."

"I dare say you could!" said Nick. "If somebody else rowed you!"

"All right," said Katie. "Laura and I will row now and you can lie back."

They changed over and Katie and Laura rowed steadily up the river while the two boys sat lazily watching the thickly-wooded banks slide past.

"Look! There's a house over there!" said

Nick suddenly. "That's the first house we've seen since we left home!"

"And what's that over by the bank?" said Katie. "Oh! It's a houseboat."

They all looked. A houseboat, badly in need of a coat of paint, was moored at the river's edge. It was very old and had been left to rot. Once it must have been a good one, with brass rails and white paint, but now it was in a dreadful state. No one could have used it for ages.

"What's that you said, a houseboat?" said Kit. "I've never seen one before. What's it for?"

"Well, it's just what its name says," said Nick. "A boat that's used as a house by its owners. They live there – cook their meals on board and sleep in bunks. A houseboat is fun. But this one can't have been lived in for years."

"I'd like to see what it's like inside," said Katie.

"Do you think it would matter if we pulled up alongside and had a look?" asked Laura.

"I don't know," said Nick. "Perhaps it belongs to the people who live at that big

house. What about going and asking permission? I'm sure they wouldn't mind."

"All right," said Katie. "You go, Nick, and take Kit."

"No, thanks," said Kit at once. "I'm not appearing in public just now!"

"Oh, I forgot!" said Katie. "Okay, I'll come with you, Nick."

They rowed to the bank near the houseboat. Nick and Katie jumped out and walked up the green lawn that led to the big house. It was shuttered, and they wondered if there was anyone there. They came to a door and knocked loudly on it.

An old woman opened it, looking most surprised. Nick felt sure she didn't have many visitors in that lonely spot!

"Excuse me," he said politely. "I just wondered if you knew about that houseboat down there? Do you think my friends and I could have a look at it?"

"I don't know anything about it," said the old woman, peering at Nick and Katie. "I'm caretaker here till the house is let. No one ever said anything to me about a houseboat. Don't you do any mischief now."

"Oh no, we won't," said Nick, and they scuttled off down the lawn. They hadn't been forbidden to look over the boat, and that was all they cared about! Nick told the others and they were delighted.

"Let's explore it straight away," said Kit. They tied their boat to a rail and then climbed up on to the deck.

There were windows and doors leading into the cabins, but they were all shut and locked. Katie peered into a window and exclaimed at what she saw.

"It's a little bedroom, with bunk beds at the side and a tiny washbasin and a hanging wardrobe and chest. Do look! It must be so exciting to live in a houseboat!"

"I've found a door where the wood has rotted round the lock!" called Kit. "We can get inside now!"

They all trooped along the wide deck to Kit. He swung open a door and the children went in. Everything was dirty, damp and spoilt, but to the four children it was marvellous. How they would like to live here! It would be great to wake up in the morning and hear the water splash against the sides of the boat, to get water from the river to fill their washbasin, and to cook a meal on the little stove in the kitchen and eat it in the open air on the deck! And how wonderful to watch the night stealing over the water, and then to go to bed on a houseboat that swayed slightly every time the river swelled a little!

"It looks as if the owner has forgotten all about this boat," said Katie. "I wish it was ours."

"Well, let's make it ours," Laura said suddenly.

"What do you mean?" asked Nick in surprise.

"Well, why shouldn't we come here and clean it up and wash the decks and polish the brass as if it were our very own boat?" said Laura. "I'm sure the owner wouldn't mind, because we would only be making the boat more valuable, not spoiling it. We could have meals here. We could even sleep here at night, if Mum said yes!"

The children stared at Laura, thinking it was a wonderful idea. A houseboat of their own! It would be amazing.

"Let's," said Kit at last. "There's nobody to stop us except the old caretaker up at the house, and she didn't even seem to know there was anything here. It can't be seen from the house, either. Let's come tomorrow and clean it up. And hey, wouldn't it make a fine hiding place for me if ever I needed one? No one would ever guess I was inside an old houseboat!"

"That's true," said Nick. "Though I don't think you'll need a hiding place, Kit, because kidnapping and things don't happen here often, but if you did, this is the place!"

"We'll bring cleaning things tomorrow and start clearing things up," said Laura. "This is going to be great. If only we could sleep here at night! How I'd love to wake up in the morning and hear the water gurgling and feel the boat rocking while I lay in my bunk."

The children thoroughly explored the houseboat. There were two bedrooms, both very small, with two bunks apiece; a tiny kitchen, hardly big enough to hold the stove and cupboards; and a small room that could be used as a sitting-room in bad weather.

The decks were big and wide, and had clearly been used for eating and sunbathing, for there were little tables and rotted deck-chairs piled under a kind of porch at the stern.

"Oh, no! It's half past four!" Kit said suddenly, in dismay. "I must get back or I'll be in deep trouble. I guess the whole household will be searching the grounds for me by now!"

"Come on, then," said Nick, scrambling back into the boat. "It won't take us long to get back if we both take an oar. Off we go! Hi, Russet, we've left you behind. Jump, silly dog, jump!"

Russet took a leap from the houseboat into the little boat and landed on Laura's lap. The boat soon left widening ripples behind it as the boys rowed strongly away.

Kit wriggled through the hole under the fencing when they got back. They could hear the loud voice of the Dragon calling for him in angry tones.

"Kit! Kit! Where are you? It's teatime. Are you asleep? Come at once!"

Kit winked at them and then gave a yell. "Hi! I'm coming! Just a minute!"

He sped up the garden, and the others went into their own house. "Tomorrow!" said Laura to Katie, rubbing her hands. "I *am* looking forward to making that boat our own!"

Chapter 9

THE *BLACK SWAN* IS CLEANED UP

The children talked a good deal about the old houseboat they'd discovered. They were all longing to go back and clean it up. "We didn't discuss with Kit when he could see us tomorrow," said Nick. "How silly of us! But we were in such a hurry to be back in time for his tea."

"Let's go tomorrow morning," said Laura. "It's Saturday, isn't it? Perhaps Kit could get the morning off. Let's ask him. Nick, you climb the tree and see if he is anywhere about. If he is, we'll throw a ball over with a message inside."

Nick climbed the tree. Kit was on the lawn next door with a book. The Dragon was nearby, reading too. Nick slithered down and told the others. He wrote a short note, stuffed it into an old split ball, and sent it over into the garden next door. In a few minutes the ball came back with an answer! It really was a very good way of sending messages.

Nick read out the note from Kit:

I'm free on Saturdays, hurray! I'll go off into the garden directly after breakfast, and hope no one will miss me till lunch-time. I'll be in your garden as near as I can to nine o'clock.

"We'll pack up some cleaning things now, shall we?" said Laura. "What's the time? Half past five. Will the shops be shut? Could we go and buy what we want? I've got some money."

"We can get the things from Aunt Marion," said Katie.

"No, we can't," said Nick. "This is a secret, remember. You can't expect Aunt Marion or anyone else to hand out soap and cloths and polish and dusters without knowing what they are for! Don't be stupid."

"I didn't think of that," said Katie. "Well, it will be much more fun to buy them, anyway. I've got some money in my money-box, too, Nick. The village shop stays open till seven. We can get our bikes and ride there."

The village was about three miles away. The children's house and Kit's were lonely places, far from anywhere, but the children had bicycles, and enjoyed cycling down to the village whenever they wanted anything. They got them out now and were soon travelling quickly along the little narrow lanes. The village shop was still open and they were able to get exactly what they wanted. They had already made out a list.

"One bottle of floor-cleaner," said Laura. "Two large floor-cloths. Two smaller cloths. A scrubbing brush. A can of polish. Three dusters. That's all." They stuffed everything into a rucksack and cycled back home, all longing to get started. They would make that old boat really beautiful!

"I wish we could paint her white, too," said Nick. "I know where there is a big tin of white paint and some brushes."

"Oh! Why don't we take those as well?" said Katie eagerly. "Then you two boys can paint the boat while Laura and I do the cleaning."

"Yes, we might take them," said Nick,

seeing in his imagination a beautiful, gleaming houseboat, painted a dazzling white, rocking gently on the river. So as soon as they got back home they went to look for the paint. They found it, along with two big brushes and some turpentine to clean the brushes if necessary.

"Quite a lot of things to carry!" said Laura, as she looked at the collection of things laid ready. "Is there anything else?"

"We'll take some chocolate and some plums and a few biscuits," said Nick. "If we start at nine and don't get back till one, we'll want something to eat." So four bars of chocolate, a packet of biscuits and a dozen or so ripe plums were put ready too.

They went to bed that night full of excitement. It was lovely to have a secret, and it was good to have a friend like Kit. They couldn't stop thinking about the old houseboat waiting for them on the river!

Just before nine o'clock the next day the three children and Russet were waiting by the hole on their side of the garden. This time Kit was punctual. He arrived exactly on the hour, and scrambled through the hole at once. Russet ran halfway down it to greet him, and licked him rapturously on the nose.

"Stop it!" said Kit, trying to turn his head away from the wet tongue as he wriggled through the hole. "Laura, call your dog off. He's awfully licky this morning, and he's been eating kippers or something."

Everyone laughed. Soon Kit was standing beside them, his eyes taking in their bulging rucksacks. "You seem to be taking a whole lot of things!" he said. "Here, let me carry yours, Katie, and I'll carry Laura's for her on the way back."

"We've got some white paint to paint up the old boat and make her smart," said Nick proudly. "Don't you think that'll be fun, Kit?"

"Great!" said Kit. "I'm a marvel at painting! Slip-slap, spatter-dash – we'll slosh the paint on that old boat in no time! Come on, let's run to your boat. I can't go slowly this morning."

They all ran across the fields to the river. They untied their boat and got in, thankfully putting down their loads. The boys took the oars. Off they went in the sunshine and didn't stop rowing until they reached the houseboat.

"There she is," said Nick as they saw her, half hidden by drooping willows. "Did anyone notice her name? I didn't."

"There it is," said Kit as they drew near. "The *Black Swan*. That's a good name, except that she must once have been a very white boat! Tie our boat up, Nick. Then we can go on board!"

The children took a look at the house in the distance. A spire of smoke came from one chimney, but otherwise it looked as deserted as it had done the day before.

"I don't think anyone is likely to disturb us," said Nick, climbing up on deck. "Give me your hand, Katie. Heave ho, there you are! Come on, Laura. Shove her up, Kit."

All four stood on the dirty decks of the *Black Swan*. They hardly knew where to begin their cleaning.

"We'll do the outside before we start on the inside," said Laura at last. "Can you boys begin to paint her white? You could do the house part first, all round the windows and wooden walls. Then you could do the doors."

"We'll wash the decks," said Katie, and got out the floor-cleaner, a scrubbing-brush and a cloth. "Wow! They really do need scrubbing. Oh, no! We forgot about a bucket for the water."

"There's probably a bucket somewhere in the tiny kitchen," said Laura, and the two girls went to see. There was one there, and another scrubbing-brush. The girls were very pleased. They dipped the bucket in the river and filled it with water. Then they set to work to scrub the dirty decks.

It was fun. The decks came beautifully clean, though they were hard to scrub. When the water was dirty the girls emptied it into the river and drew up some fresh water. It was even easier than turning on a tap!

Meanwhile the two boys were splashing about with the white paint. Kit was right, he did know about painting things, and he showed Nick how to lay the white paint evenly. The piece they had done looked really good.

The girls cleaned the windows and then tried to polish the brass rails round the deck, but these were really too tarnished. By this time it was eleven o'clock and the children were tired and hungry.

"Let's sit down and have biscuits and chocolate," said Nick. So down they sat on the clean deck, and began to munch happily.

"The walls you've painted do look nice," said Katie to the boys. "And the decks look better now they're clean, don't they? Laura and I had better start on the inside of the cabins after we've had a rest. Everything's in a mess there. We'll bring out some of the cushions and things to air. They smell damp."

The children worked very hard indeed at cleaning and tidying the houseboat. Laura and Katie opened all the doors and windows of the boat and let the breeze blow through to take the musty dampness away. By the time that half past twelve came and they had to go, the boat was beginning to look very different.

"Goodbye, *Black Swan!*" said Katie as they rowed away. "We'll come again soon, tomorrow, perhaps."

They were all late for lunch, because they hadn't really left themselves enough time to get back. They knew Laura's mother wouldn't mind, but it was different for Kit. Nobody must know that he had escaped from his garden. If his secret was discovered, the hole would be filled in, and he would never be able to play with Nick and the others again.

"Bye!" said the boy, disappearing into the hole. "See you tomorrow!"

Chapter 10

LAURA'S BIRTHDAY CAKE AND A SURPRISE

Kit couldn't go with the children when they next went to visit their houseboat. Mr Barton, his tutor, was keeping rather a strict eye on him, because the Dragon had complained that he had hidden himself in the garden and wouldn't come when he was called. Actually, of course, Kit had been out on the river, and hadn't heard anyone calling him! But he couldn't very well explain that.

Nick, Katie and Laura went on with the cleaning and painting without him. Before another week had gone by it looked really lovely. It was dazzling white, and the brass had actually begun to shine a little! The windows were bright, the little stove shone, all the crockery was washed, and the cushions well pummelled to rid them of dust.

"We ought to give a party!" said Laura,

looking at the houseboat proudly. "We could get out the little red tables and chairs from the back of the boat and use those."

"A party! Who for?" asked Nick. "There's nobody to give a party for."

"We could give one for ourselves," said Laura. "It's my birthday next week. I don't see why we couldn't have my birthday here, cake and all. It would be fantastic!"

"It's a great idea," said Nick. "Let's ask your mother if we can take a birthday tea out. We can ask Kit to come as well."

So when Laura's birthday came, four children and a dog went to the cleaned-up houseboat and climbed on to its spotless decks. Nick had the birthday cake in a tin. "There are twelve candles in the tin, too," he said. "They're loose, we can stick them on the cake when we're ready. There are chocolate biscuits too, and three different kinds of sandwiches."

Kit had managed to get the afternoon off. Both his tutor and Miss Taylor had gone out. Then he had wriggled through the hole and joined the others, who were impatiently waiting for him. Russet gave a welcoming yelp.

When they got to the houseboat, the children set out the pretty tables and chairs. They put the food on them and fetched mugs and plates from the tiny kitchen.

Laura had a look at the little stove. What a pity they couldn't make some tea!

"Not that we really want tea to drink," she thought, "because we've got lemonade. It would be fun to boil a kettle on the stove, though. One day we'll bring some water with us and make tea or cocoa."

The others called her. "Laura, what are you doing? Do come on! We want to begin."

The birthday cake had been taken out of its tin and put on a big plate in the middle of one of the tables. It looked lovely. Laura's mother had set twelve pink and white roses round it, to hold the twelve candles. Nick carefully put them into the rose holders.

"There!" he said. "That looks lovely! When shall we light the candles, Laura?"

"Now," said Laura. "They won't show much in the open air, but we must light them."

But unfortunately nobody had any

matches, so the candles couldn't be lit. It was a great pity.

"I do hate to cut the cake without lighting the candles first," said Laura sadly. "I'll see if there are any matches in the little kitchen." She disappeared into the kitchen and rummaged about. She came out smiling. "I've got a box," she said. "They were in that tiny cupboard by the larder. You light the candles, Nick, please."

But the matches were so damp and old that they wouldn't strike. The children sat at the little tables, disappointedly striking matches that wouldn't light, and getting quite cross about it. Russet watched everything with the greatest interest. He couldn't think why the children didn't stop fussing about candles and cut the cake. He knew dogs at birthday parties usually got a share!

"We'll just have to cut the cake without lighting the candles, that's all," said Nick at last. "Now, remember, everyone, you must wish when you eat your first bit of cake. Birthday-cake wishes are magic, and always come true!"

Suddenly Russet sat up straight and

growled. The children looked at him in astonishment.

"Russet, what are you growling for?" asked Laura. "Are you cross because you haven't got a bit of my cake yet? You are an impatient dog!"

Russet growled again, and the children saw that all the hairs on the back of his neck were standing up. They did that when Russet was angry. But what could he be angry about?

Russet was staring through the drooping willow trees that hid the houseboat. Was somebody coming? The children couldn't hear anyone. But then footsteps over grass wouldn't be heard. Nobody wanted to be caught on the houseboat because, although they felt it was theirs now they had cleaned and painted it so beautifully, they knew it really wasn't.

"Listen," said Kit in a low voice. "If it's anybody snooping round, don't give me away. I shall have to pretend to be dumb, because everybody knows I'm an American as soon as I open my mouth. I can't talk the way you do. And so if anyone—"

He stopped short and stared between the

trees. He had seen something moving there. Someone was walking on the bank!

"Let's hope they won't see us," whispered Nick. "Laura, make Russet be quiet. He's going to growl again."

Laura put her hand on Russet's collar. He stopped rumbling inside at once. He knew when he had to be quiet! They all sat as still as mice. They heard a little cough behind the trees. They could see no one yet, and felt certain that no one could see them.

Then a tall man with blue eyes appeared on the bank where the willows ended, staring at the houseboat! He stared at the boat and at the children in the greatest astonishment. They stared back. They didn't know what to say or do, so they just stared. Russet gave a growl.

"Well, well, well!" said the man at last, and he stepped on board the houseboat. "Quite a nice little party! A birthday party, too, by the look of that magnificent cake!"

Still nobody said a word. The man took a look round the decks and popped his head in at the sitting-room and bedroom windows of the boat. He seemed more surprised than ever.

"I suppose none of you has a tongue?" he said, sitting down in an empty chair. "If you had, I should love to ask you a few questions."

"We have got tongues," said Nick. "What do you want to ask us?"

"Well, I'd love to know what you are doing on my old houseboat," said the man, and the children listened in dismay. His houseboat! What bad luck that they had chosen that day to come!

"And I'd love to know who gave the old *Black Swan* a dazzling coat of paint," said the man. "And who cleaned up the rooms inside. Most mysterious. I suppose you don't know the answer to these questions?"

Nick couldn't help rather liking the man, though he also wondered if by any chance he could be that wicked uncle of Kit's. Just suppose he was!

"Is it your boat?" he said. "I'm very sorry if we're trespassing. I did ask permission from the caretaker at the house to go over the boat, but she didn't seem to know anything about it. We haven't done any damage. We just gave her a coat of paint and cleaned her up a bit. We thought she was rather nice, you see, and we didn't like to see her falling to bits."

"I quite agree with you," said the man. "Well, I must say you are different from most children I know. They would do as much damage as they could but you seem to have gone out of your way to put my boat in good order. What are your names?"

"I'm Nick," said Nick, "and this is my sister Katie, and that's Laura, who's having the birthday."

"And who are you?" said the man, turning to Kit who, of course, had not said a word the whole time, but had tried to look as dumb and stupid as possible.

Kit stared at the man and didn't answer.

"That's Sam," said Nick, saying the first name that came into his head. "You won't be able to make him speak. He's dumb."

"Poor lad!" said the man, and he really did look sorry. "I wonder if anything could be done for you. I'm a doctor, and I might be able to help you."

"There's nothing that can be done for him," said Nick hastily. He didn't want the man trying any cure on poor Kit. "Well, we'd better clear up and go, since it's your boat. We're sorry if we've trespassed, as I said before."

"Well, of course you have trespassed," said the man. "But it's what I would call very satisfactory trespassing from my point of view – very!"

He smiled and the children were relieved to see him looking so good-tempered. "I suppose," said Nick, smiling also, "I suppose you wouldn't let us trespass again, would you?"

"Well, I might, on one condition," said the man. "And that is that you ask me to your party and give me a piece of that delicious-looking cake. Why don't you light the candles?"

"We've no matches," said Laura.

The man took out a box and handed it to her. She struck a match and lit the twelve candles. Then she cut the cake. She gave a piece first to the man. "Here you are, Mr – Mr . . ." she said.

"My name is Cunningham," said the man. "Thank you, Laura. Many happy returns of the day and please treat my houseboat as yours whenever you like! I will rent it to you for one piece of birthday cake!"

What a bit of luck! The children stared at one another in delight. So the *Black Swan* would be theirs whenever they liked!

Chapter 11

WHO IS DUMB SAM?

Mr Cunningham ate his piece of cake and said it was the best he had ever tasted.

"Did you wish?" asked Laura. "You have to wish, you know."

"I did," said Mr Cunningham. "Where do you live, by the way? I didn't know there were any houses nearby."

"There aren't. Only that one over there," said Nick. "We live in one of the two houses down the river. We came here in our boat. Where do you live?"

"I used to live in that house beyond the lawn there," said the man, nodding towards the house in the distance. "But now I want to let it, and I think I have let it, so that's lucky for me."

"Will the people want the houseboat?" asked Katie in dismay.

"No. I thought it had fallen to bits, so I didn't mention it," said the man. "You needn't worry. The boat will be nothing to do with them. You can say you have rented it from me if anyone asks you. And I must say it was very good rent you paid me – a most delicious piece of cake!"

"Have another bit?" said Laura, taking up the knife.

"Well, if I do, that must be rent for two years," said Mr Cunningham. "Thanks very much."

All this time Kit had been munching his cake and saying nothing.

Mr Cunningham glanced at him. "Has he always been unable to speak?" he asked.

Nick went red. He hardly knew what to say. He was a truthful boy, but he couldn't possibly give Kit away. "Well, not always," he said at last.

Laura saw that Nick was feeling awkward, and she hurriedly changed the subject. "Have another bit of cake, Sam?" she asked.

Katie wanted to giggle when she heard Laura calling Kit "Sam". Kit made a curious noise in his throat and took another piece of cake.

"Is that all the noise he can make?" said

Mr Cunningham. The others thought of the fearsome yells and whoops that Kit could make when he wanted to.

"No, he can make other noises," said Nick. "Have a biscuit, sir?"

"No, thanks! I must be off," said Mr Cunningham, and got up. "Well, thank you very much for two years' rent, and remember, you are welcome to use my boat whenever you want to. Goodbye!"

"Goodbye," said everyone except Kit, who made another curious noise in his throat. Russet gave a polite yelp. He had quite taken to their visitor.

They all watched the man walk away and disappear behind the trees. Then Katie giggled.

"Poor Sam!" she said. "I do feel sorry for you. Are you awfully dumb?"

Kit made a few noises and the others shouted with laughter. Then Kit grinned and found his tongue.

"Thanks for playing up so well," he said. "I think that man is perfectly all right, but you never know when any of my wicked uncle's spies might come around. Anyway, if Mr Cunningham is one, he won't think that a dumb boy called Sam is Christopher Anthony Armstrong, who is anything but dumb!"

"I don't think he is anybody horrible," said Laura. "I thought he was nice, especially letting us have the boat in return for two pieces of cake. Grown-ups do do funny things, don't they?"

"Well, we got the candles lit anyway," said Katie. "Look, they've all burned down now. Blow them out, Laura."

Laura blew and the candles went out.

"You're a good blower," said Kit, feeling his head. "Is my hair still on?"

They all laughed. They felt very pleased to think that they hadn't got into trouble over the boat, and the thought that it was theirs to do as they liked with was brilliant! What fun they would have!

"Do you think Aunt Marion would let us spend a night here?" Katie said suddenly. "Wouldn't it be fantastic?"

"Well, we'd have to tell her about the boat then," said Nick. "But it won't matter now, because we've got permission to use it. She might let us come here for a night, or even a weekend."

"What about Kit?" said Laura. The boy's eyes had begun to sparkle at the thought of a night on the boat.

"Oh, I'd slip off late at night and get back early in the morning," said Kit at once. "You don't suppose I'd be left out of an adventure like that, do you? But, listen, I must get back now, or the Dragon will complain about me to Mr Barton. I don't want to be locked up in my bedroom or anything awful like that."

The children cleared everything away and then got into their little boat. They rowed off, very pleased with their afternoon. Luckily Kit got back in time and no one knew he had escaped for the afternoon. Laura gave him another piece of her birthday cake to smuggle up to his bedroom.

"You ask your mother about sleeping a night on the boat," he said. "We'll do that as soon as we can, while the fine weather lasts. And ask your mother if she's ever heard of Mr Cunningham. If he did used to live at that house, he must be all right."

So the children told Mrs Greyling all about Mr Cunningham and his houseboat.

She listened in amazement when she heard how they had discovered the boat and painted it and cleaned it.

"But you shouldn't have done that! You might have got into serious trouble, you know. It was very nice of Mr Cunningham to say you can go there again."

"Do you know him, Aunt Marion?" asked Katie.

"I've heard of him," said Mrs Greyling. "He used to live at the house there, but now I think he's trying to let it."

"He told us he has let it," said Nick. "But the people aren't going to have the houseboat. Aunt Marion, can we spend a night there? Please let us!"

"Well, I'll have to find out if Mr Cunningham really means what he said," said Mrs Greyling. "I'll go and telephone him now. I think I can find his number."

She went off to telephone. The children looked at one another delightedly.

"I bet we'll be allowed to sleep on board!" said Nick. "How fantastic! Think of having breakfast there, and cooking bacon and eggs on that little stove!"

The children could almost smell the

bacon and eggs already. They waited impatiently for their mother to come back. She soon came into the room again, but she looked rather puzzled.

"Yes, it seems quite all right," she said. "Mr Cunningham was amused at finding you having a birthday party on the boat, and pleased that you had painted and cleaned it so nicely, but he said something about a boy called Sam, who couldn't speak."

The children looked at one another in dismay. What bad luck that Mr Cunningham had mentioned Kit! Now what were they to say? They said nothing, and hoped Mrs Greyling would say no more.

"Who is this Sam?" she asked. "And why have you never told me about him? Is he really dumb? What's he like, and where did you meet him?"

"He's just a boy," said Nick at last. "He's about as old as I am. We met him, that's all."

"Mr Cunningham says he's dumb," went on Mrs Greyling. "He's a doctor, and he wondered if he could have anything done for him. He thought he was your brother or cousin, it seems."

"Oh!" said Nick.

Mrs Greyling looked at him impatiently. "I shall begin to think you're dumb next!" she said. "Where does this boy live?"

This was a most awkward question but very fortunately Russet changed the subject so completely that nobody had to answer. Tiger the cat happened to come into the room at that moment, and Russet saw her. With an excited yelp he jumped at her, and in a moment there was a regular circus in the sitting-room! Tiger climbed up the curtains to escape and Russet leaped like a mad thing after her, knocking down everything that got in his way. Mrs Greyling shouted, and Laura yelled.

Then Tiger decided that she had had enough. She jumped on top of Russet and put out her claws. She dug eight sharp needles into him, and he yelled with pain. He turned himself about and ran to hide behind Laura, but Tiger came after him.

Poor Russet! He ran out of the door with Tiger chasing him for all she was worth. She leaped at his back and dug her claws into him again. He ran upstairs and she ran after him. He tore downstairs and she tore after him. Into the sitting-room again and all round it, between everyone's legs went the two excited animals.

Somehow or other Laura caught Russet and Katie shut the door on Tiger.

"Well, really!" Laura's mother said, sinking into a chair. "It's bad enough when a dog chases a cat but it's far worse when a cat chases a dog. Laura, go and put Russet into his basket up in your room and shut the door on him. I don't want to see him again for at least two hours."

The children went out of the room with Russet, and heaved a sigh of relief.

"Tiger came in at just the right moment!" said Nick. "I really don't know what I could have said about Kit. I do hope Aunt Marion forgets about him."

She did, which was very lucky. She asked no more questions at all, but simply said that if they were really good for the next few days she would let them spend a night on the houseboat!

"We must tell Kit!" said Katie. "Won't he be excited!"

Chapter 12

Is it the Wicked Uncle?

The children talked of nothing else but going to spend a night on the houseboat.

"There are two little bedrooms, with two bunks in each," said Nick. "Just right for the four of us. Russet can sleep with one of us in a bunk."

"With me, of course," said Laura. "You don't suppose he'd sleep with anyone else, do you? Won't it be fun undressing at night in the cabins? We'll have to light candles to see by."

"We'll get that stove going," said Nick. "And we must remember to get water for the kettle. We can't drink river water."

"I should think the old caretaker would let us have some water," said Laura. "We could tell her that Mr Cunningham said we could use the boat."

"Yes, that would save us having to take water with us," said Nick. "We'll get Aunt

Marion to give us bacon and eggs and bread and anything else we want."

Laura's mother said they could go the following Friday. They slipped next door and told Kit, who was thrilled.

"I'll have to join you there," he said. "I won't be able to go out of any of the downstairs doors because they are always locked and bolted at night, and if I went out and left one unbolted, as I would have to do, Mr Barton would be certain to discover it the next morning. He often gets up early to work. So I'll slip out of the attic window, across the plank and down the ash tree."

"What! In the dark?" said Laura.

"It won't be dark," said Kit. "There'll be some kind of a moon. Anyway, I could do it in the dark, easily."

"Can you come for a picnic with us tomorrow?" asked Nick. "We're going to take our tea to Bracken Hill. We can lend you a bike."

"I'd love to," said Kit. "But I can't. Both the Dragon and Mr Barton will be in to tea tomorrow, and I'll have to be there. I can't keep on and on disappearing for meals."

"What a pity!" said Nick. "Never mind, you can look forward to a night on the boat."

"I sure will!" said Kit. "Watch out, here's the Dragon!"

The fierce woman came across the lawn. All the children were at the back of the summerhouse, behind a bush. The Dragon called Kit.

"Kit! I want you to do something for me. Where are you?"

Kit appeared, whistling.

The Dragon sat down in the deck-chair and said, "Could you go indoors and find my book for me? I left it behind."

Kit went indoors. The other children stood still behind the summerhouse, hardly daring to breathe. Russet stood perfectly still, too. He really was a very good dog.

Kit appeared again. He caught sight of Nick peering anxiously from behind the summerhouse and winked at him.

"Here you are, Miss Taylor," he said, and he held out a book. Miss Taylor gave a grunt of annoyance.

"That's not it," she said. "That belongs to Mr Barton. Dear me, what a stupid boy you can be at times. I suppose I'd better go and look for it, or you'll bring me out your own book next!"

And, to the children's great relief, the Dragon got up and walked towards the house.

"Good for you, Kit!" whispered Nick, and the three children and Russet moved off quickly into the little wood beyond the lawn. It wasn't long before they were scrambling down the hole to safety.

"It's a pity Kit can't come tomorrow," said Nick. "Never mind, we three will go."

The children had a lovely picnic and ate every single thing they had brought with them. Then they wandered about looking for early blackberries, but there were very few.

"I'm jolly thirsty," said Nick, mopping his hot forehead. "Have we drunk all the lemonade?"

"Every drop," said Laura. "Can't we go and buy some more?"

"I've got some money," said Nick, feeling in his pocket. So they got on their bicycles and set off to the village nearby. It stood where three roads met, and had several shops that sold soft drinks and ice creams.

They went into the biggest shop and sat down at a little table, meaning to have a drink, and some ice creams too. As they sat there, a big car drove up outside and a man got out. He came into the shop.

"Excuse me," he said to the woman there. "Could you tell me if I'm anywhere near Faldham?"

"Not far," said the woman. "Take the middle road, sir."

"How far is it in miles?" asked the man.

"About eight miles, I'd say," said the woman, taking the three children their drinks and ices.

Katie spoke up at once. "It's not as much as eight," she said. "I've measured it on the speedometer of my bike. It's exactly six and a half."

"Do you live at Faldham, by any chance?" asked the man, coming over to the children.

"We live outside Faldham," said Nick.

The man sat down and ordered an ice for himself. "Bit of a lonely spot, isn't it?" he asked.

"Yes, very," said Laura. "There are only

two houses outside the village, ours and another close by."

"Who lives there?" asked the man, eating his ice.

"I don't really know," said Laura. Then she got such a kick on the ankle from Nick that she nearly swallowed the spoon with which she was ladling ice cream into her mouth!

"Has anybody new moved in lately?" asked the man, but by this time Laura was choking over her swallowed ice cream.

Nick answered: "The houses are very far apart with thick hedges between so it's difficult to see what goes on next door. A family of aliens may have arrived, for all we know!"

"Ha, ha!" said the man, laughing as if he didn't really think it was a funny joke at all. "You don't happen to have seen a small boy around there, do you?"

"How small?" asked Nick solemnly, scraping round his bowl.

"Small as you," said the man.

"I'm big," said Nick.

"Well, as big as you!" said the man impatiently.

"What colour eyes?" asked Nick.

"Blue," said the man.

"What colour hair?" said Nick.

"Fair," said the man.

"How many fingers?" said Nick, again very solemnly. The man stared at him with annoyance.

"Do you think you're being funny?" he asked at last.

"Yes, I do rather," said Nick, and Katie and Laura gave explosive little giggles. The man got up impatiently.

"I'll send you a message if I see a small,

big boy with blue eyes, fair hair, and – how many fingers did you say?" asked Nick.

"Don't be rude," said the man shortly. He paid his bill and drove off in his car.

"Phew!" said Nick, letting out a big sigh of relief. "I bet you anything you like that's the wicked uncle! And somehow or other he's found out that Kit is in our district. We'll have to warn Kit. Oh, no, that'll mean he'll have to go off somewhere else and hide! I say, Laura, I really thought you were going to give the game away. I'm sorry I kicked you so hard."

"It's all right," said Laura. "You only made me choke. I didn't for one moment think that man was after Kit. I do hope he won't find him."

"Come on – we must get back and warn him," said Nick, standing up. "Put Russet into your basket."

Off they all went again, rushing back to warn Kit of danger. What a strange thing that they had happened to be in the shop when his wicked uncle came by!

Chapter 13

An Unwelcome Visitor

The children rode home quickly, glancing nervously at the sky, which looked grey enough for rain.

"Did you have a nice picnic?" called Mrs Greyling.

"Lovely!" said Laura.

"Come and tell me all about it," said her mother. But that was just what the children didn't want to do! They wanted to warn Kit as quickly as possible.

"You two girls go in and talk to Aunt Marion, and I'll slip under the fence and tell Kit," said Nick in a low voice.

So the girls went to tell her all about the picnic, and Nick slipped out of the garden door and down to the hole under the fencing. He crawled underneath and stood up in the next door garden. He wondered where Kit was.

It was raining a little by now, so he

thought Kit was probably in his attic room. He decided to go up and see. Carefully he made his way all round the grounds, keeping in the thick bushes and trees, and at last came to where the garage backed on to the house. The ladder to get up to the roof was not there, but it only took Nick a couple of minutes to get it from the empty garage. He set it against the wall, climbed up, stood on the flat garage roof and then swung himself into the branches of the big ash tree nearby. Up he went like a cat, and came level with the attic window.

He gave a low whistle, rather like a blackbird. No answer. He whistled again, and this time Kit's head appeared at the window. He grinned in delight when he saw Nick.

"Hey, great!" he said. "Come in."

Nick slid along the plank that stretched from the sill to the tree, and jumped down into the big attic. Kit locked the door.

Nick spoke in a low voice. "Kit, I believe that wicked uncle of yours is in the district!"

"Don't be crazy!" said Kit. "He couldn't possibly know I'm here yet."

"Well, listen," said Nick and he told Kit about the man in the big car, and the questions he had asked.

"Hey! It does sound a bit strange," said Kit. "Thanks for being clever enough not to give me away. What was the man like?"

"Fairly tall, fair hair, a bit like yours, very blue eyes," said Nick. "But you've never seen your uncle, have you?"

"No," said Kit. "Although he has kidnapped me twice, he's always used other people to do the dirty work. But it looks as though there's a family resemblance between us, doesn't it? Rats! I did think I was going to settle down here for some time. It's been such fun being with you. Now, shall I tell Mr Barton and the Dragon, or not?"

"I think you ought to," said Nick. "Listen, is that your tutor's car coming back?"

They both went to the window and Nick gave a cry of alarm. "Oh no! That's the same car the man was in this afternoon! But he's gone past your house and he's turning in to our house!"

"Strange," said Kit. "You'd better go

back and find out what he says, Nick."

So Nick hurriedly went back down the tree, through the hole, and up his garden. He rushed into the house and bumped into the man in the hall, where he was talking to Mrs Greyling.

"Hello!" said the man. "Here's the rude boy again!"

"Rude?" Mrs Greyling said in astonishment. "Nick, have you been rude?"

Nick felt most uncomfortable. He stood and said nothing. The man looked at Mrs Greyling.

"I am looking for a boy who is supposed to be in this district," he said. "I'm very, very anxious to find him. I thought perhaps he might be in this house or the next one, as these seem to be the only two around."

"Well, there's only Nick here," said Mrs Greyling. "I don't know of any other boy. I am sure there isn't one next door. But wait, there is another boy!"

"Really?" said the man. "Where is he? What is he like?"

"Well, I've never seen him myself," said Mrs Greyling. "I know two things about him that might perhaps help you. His name

122

is Sam and the poor boy can't speak. He's dumb."

"I'm afraid he's not the boy I'm after," said the man. "The boy I want is called Christopher Anthony Armstrong, known as Kit. You're sure you haven't heard of another boy anywhere here?"

"Well, there are only these two houses here," said Mrs Greyling. "I would certainly know if any boy was living nearby. If Sam isn't the boy you want, I'm afraid you won't find him in Faldham."

"Well, thank you very much," said the man. "I must have been mistaken. But, madam, I'd take it as a very kind act on your part if you'd telephone this number if you hear of any boy of thirteen years old called Kit Armstrong."

"Very well," said Mrs Greyling, feeling quite puzzled, and taking the man's card as he spoke. "I'm sorry my boy was rude to you. It's most unlike him."

"Oh, that's all right," said the man, going out of the front door and getting into his car. He then drove off without calling at Kit's house at all.

"Nick! What does this mean? Were you

really rude to that man?" asked Mrs Greyling, shocked. "What happened?"

"Well, he just asked me a lot of questions, and I didn't see why I should answer them," said Nick, rather sulkily. "I didn't like him."

"You mustn't be rude to strangers just because you don't like them," said Mrs Greyling. "I really do feel ashamed of you. I'm sorry I couldn't help the man, he seemed quite concerned about this boy called Kit. I didn't like to ask him why he was so anxious to find him."

Nick could have told her, but he didn't want to. He hurried off to find the two girls and tell them that the man had actually come to call on Mrs Greyling. They listened in horror.

"Oh dear," said Laura. "I suppose Kit will have to go soon."

"I don't see why," said Katie. "After all, now the man won't think that Kit is staying anywhere around here, so he'll probably go and look somewhere else! It would be best for Kit to stay where he is. The man won't come looking in the same place twice!"

"You're right, Katie," said Nick, cheering

up. "Quite right! If he doesn't come back within a day or two, we'll tell Kit not to say anything to the Dragon or to Mr Barton, but just to sit tight and hope the man won't appear any more, but will go hunting in other places called Faldham!"

"That man talked like an American," said Laura thoughtfully. "But he didn't look very wicked, did he?"

"Why should wicked people look wicked?" said Nick. "You can't tell. Anyway, he must be Kit's uncle, because he's very like him."

Nick and the girls didn't manage to tell Kit what had happened that evening. Laura's mother insisted that, as it was raining, they all stay inside and play a game. Meanwhile, Kit was feeling rather anxious, wondering what had happened. Why had the man gone next door?

At bedtime, when they were undressing, a shower of little stones rattled against the windows. Nick jumped, and then went to look out. In the garden below was Kit! He signalled to Nick to discover if he was alone.

"It's all right," said Nick, leaning out of

the window. Kit climbed up the pear tree by the wall, and was soon astride the windowsill. The girls came into the room, and Kit was told all about the man's visit.

"He really is after you, there's no doubt about that," said Nick. "But Aunt Marion put him right off, though she didn't know it! We think he'll go off to another Faldham now. There are seven other places called Faldham, you know, and I'm sure he won't come back here. So don't you think it would be best not to say a word to Mr Barton or the Dragon till we see if there's any further sign of the man?"

"Anyway, if there is, you can always hide on the houseboat!" said Laura, her eyes shining.

Kit nodded. "I shan't say a word," he decided. "Not a word. And, as you say, I can always rush off to the houseboat. Nobody would ever guess I was there! Thanks very much, all of you. Now I must go, or the Dragon will come after me with smoke and flames pouring out of her nostrils!"

The children giggled as Kit slid down the pear tree. Just as he landed, Mrs Greyling happened to draw the curtains downstairs, and gazed in astonishment at the dark shadow dropping to the ground.

"Nick!" she called. "Is that you? You naughty boy, what are you doing?"

Nick heard her and groaned. "Oh, no! Now Aunt Marion will know there was someone here tonight. The cat will be out of the bag."

"You drop down the tree quickly," said Katie, "and then climb up again. You'll get into the bedroom just as Aunt Marion comes in, and she'll never guess it was Kit. Quick!"

The two girls shot out of the room. Nick dropped down the tree and then climbed up again, appearing at the window as Mrs Greyling came into the room.

"Nick! So it was you! What do you mean by behaving like this when you are supposed to be in bed?"

"I'm very sorry, Aunt Marion," said Nick humbly, and got into bed.

"I should think so!" she said, and turned the light out with a click. Really, what would these children be up to next?

Chapter 14

OFF FOR A NIGHT ON THE BOAT

The children were very busy preparing for Friday. Mrs Greyling said they were to take rugs with them, because she felt sure the bedding would be damp.

"You must spread each bunk with a rug," she said. "And be sure to drag the bedding out into the hot sun to give it another airing before you sleep on it. Now, what do you want to take with you to eat?"

"Oh, heaps of things," said Nick. "You've got no idea how hungry we get on the river, Aunt Marion!"

"Well, I can guess," she said, with a laugh. "All right. I'll pack lots of food for you and you can put it in your rucksacks so there'll be no problem about carrying it. You'll have plenty of other things to take too. Don't forget your pyjamas, towels and toothbrushes."

There were so many things to take just

for one night on the boat! But it was decided that they should leave some things there for another time.

"It looks as if we'll often be able to spend the night there," said Nick. "I hope Kit will, too. I miss him when he doesn't come. Laura, are you taking dog biscuits for Russet?"

"Of course!" said Laura.

"Don't forget his toothbrush and pyjamas," said Katie solemnly.

"Idiot!" said Laura. "Russet, will you enjoy spending a night with us on a boat?"

"Woof," said Russet, and wagged his tail joyously. He was happy to be anywhere with the children.

The day came at last, sunny and hot. The children were sorry to set off without Kit, but he did not dare to escape from the Dragon until night-time.

"I'll go to bed early, though," he promised, "and then I'll be able to come about nine, I hope. Will you come and fetch me in the boat, Nick? It's a bore for you to have to come all the way back for me, but I can't think what else to do. I could follow the riverbank till I come to the houseboat, but I guess I'd have to go a good bit out of my way at times."

"Yes, you would," said Nick. "Of course I'll come and fetch you in the boat. I'll be waiting at our usual place at nine o'clock. It'll be getting dark then. No one will see you."

The three children and Russet set off in the early afternoon, rucksacks on their backs and carrying a couple of rugs. They were very excited at the thought of sleeping on the boat in the bunk beds.

"We'll go to bed quite late," said Nick. "For one thing, I won't be back until at least half past nine with Kit, then we'll want to talk."

They arrived at the boat and all the children began to pile the goods into it. Then Nick took the oars and they set off. The afternoon sun shining down on them was very hot indeed.

"First thing is to have a swim when we arrive," said Katie. "I must get cool somehow!"

They came to the white-painted houseboat and clambered up the side. Nick handed the things to the girls, and they piled them on the deck, ready to be sorted out. Then he tied the boat to the *Black Swan* and clambered on board too.

"We'd better put the bedding out into the sun," he said.

"Oh, let's swim first," said Katie. "I'm so hot."

"No, we might forget about the bedding," said Nick. "Come on. We promised."

So, before anything else was done, all the bedding from the four bunks was dragged out and strewn over the decks in the hot sun.

"It'll be absolutely baked!" said Nick. "I'm sure it won't have a scrap of dampness left in it. Now shall we swim?"

"Yes," said Laura. "I'll just put the milk into the little larder in a bucket of water to keep it cool. And put the food out of the sun, Nick, will you? We'll arrange everything after we've swum."

It was lovely to be in the cool river water, and when eventually the children had had enough, they climbed on to the deck of the *Black Swan* and lay drying themselves in the sun. "What about a drink?" said Katie.

"I'm dreadfully thirsty now."

"Get it yourself, then," said Nick. "I can't move."

"Nor can I!" said Laura dreamily. "Can you feel the boat moving up and down a little as the river flows beneath it? Isn't it marvellous? I do love this old boat."

The children lay there lazily for half an hour and then got up to arrange their things and get some tea. It was fun choosing their bunks. The girls had one little bedroom, and Nick put his things on one of the bunks in the other. "Kit will bring his own things, I expect," he said. He stuck new candles into the candlesticks, and put matches there, too. All the children were secretly looking forward to the night-time.

The girls unpacked the food and put it neatly into the tiny larder. Then they set tea on one of the little red tables outside in the sunshine.

"There's plenty of lemonade to drink," said Katie. "But when we have supper tonight, we'll boil water to make some cocoa. That'll be fun."

"We'll have to go and ask the old

caretaker for some water, then," said Nick. "Hope she won't mind!"

"You go, Nick," said Katie. "She's seen you before. Take the kettle with you."

So, at about six o'clock, Nick took the kettle from the little stove and set off up the lawn to where the big house stood in the distance. Smoke curled up from a chimney so the boy knew there was someone there. He wondered idly if the new people had arrived yet, the ones to whom Mr Cunningham had let the house. There seemed no sign of them.

He went round to the back door and knocked. No one answered. He knocked again, more loudly, and then pushed the door. The old caretaker was working in the kitchen there. She looked up with a jump when she saw Nick.

"Bless us all!" she said, annoyed. "What do you mean by making me jump like that? What do you want?"

"Please would you be good enough to let me have some water for my kettle?" asked Nick politely.

"Why? Are you picnicking anywhere here?" asked the old woman. "You'd better not! Mr Cunningham has let the house now, and the people are here already. You'll get into trouble if you trespass in these grounds."

"It's all right," said Nick. "We're in the old houseboat on the river."

"Oh, is that the houseboat you spoke about the other day when you came?" said the caretaker. "I haven't had time to go down and have a look at it yet. I've been so busy getting ready for the new people. But you'd better be careful about using that houseboat. You might be turned off it!"

"No, we shan't," said Nick. "May I get the water, please?"

"There's a tap you can use just outside the kitchen door," said the old woman. "Use it when you like, and don't come bothering me any more."

"All right," said Nick. "I'm sorry to have disturbed you. I won't again. I'll just get the water when I want it."

He shut the kitchen door and went to find the tap outside. There was one just under the kitchen window. As Nick went to fill his kettle, he heard a man's voice speaking to the old woman in sharp tones.

"Who was that here just now?"

"A boy," said the caretaker.

"Where does he come from?" said the voice. "I don't want children messing about here. We came here to be perfectly quiet and private."

"He said something about being on the houseboat at the bottom of the garden," muttered the caretaker crossly. "You'd better ask him yourself where he comes from. I don't know anything about him."

"A houseboat at the bottom of the garden!" said the man's voice in surprise. "I haven't heard anything about that. That must belong to the property, then. I'll have a look at it. Mr Cunningham must have forgotten to tell me about it. It might be useful when I want to work by myself."

Nick heard all this in dismay. He hoped the man wouldn't make any difficulties about the houseboat. It would be a bore if they had to tie it up somewhere else. He wondered if he should have a word with the man, but as there was silence after that, it was clear that he had left the kitchen. Perhaps he wouldn't bother any more about the boat.

"Anyway, Mr Cunningham rented it to us!" thought Nick as he sped off with kettle. "That man can't turn us out! I hope he won't come down to the *Black Swan* tonight!"

But that was just what he did do!

Chapter 15

A NASTY SHOCK

Nick went back to the houseboat and told the girls what he had overheard. They were all very worried. It would be awful to be turned off the boat just as they had planned to spend the night there.

"I hope the man doesn't come tonight while you're away fetching Kit," said Laura.

"Oh, he'll come before dark, if he's coming," said Nick. "I'll be here. You needn't worry. After all, so long as we've got permission from the owner, that's all that matters!"

But somehow the evening was a bit spoiled.

At about half past seven, when the water was purple with the long shadows of trees in the evening sunshine, the children heard voices in the distance. Russet pricked up his ears and growled a little.

"Oh," said Laura, looking worried, "do

you think it's someone coming to the boat?"

It was! The voices came nearer, and then two men appeared at the side of the drooping willows that hid the boat. They didn't look at all pleasant. In fact, they looked as stern as the Dragon. The children looked at them and said nothing.

"What are you kids doing here?" said one man in a sharp voice. He had cold eyes and short fair hair. The other man was smaller and dark.

"We're spending the night on this houseboat," said Nick politely.

"Oh no, you're not!" said the man. "You're going to clear out of here in double-quick time! We've rented this property, and we're not having any kids messing about. This houseboat belongs to us!"

"It doesn't," said Nick boldly. "It's been rented to us."

This was quite true, but the man didn't believe a word. He gave a short laugh. "And what rent do you pay?" he asked in a scornful voice. Nobody answered.

"Well, speak up!" said the man. "I suppose you're lying, so you can't answer.

Well, clear up your things and be gone in half an hour."

This was too much for Katie. "We've paid our rent, for two whole years!" she said indignantly. "You just ask Mr Cunningham!"

"And what rent did you pay?" said the

man mockingly. "Two pence a week?"

"No, we paid Mr Cunningham two slices of Laura's birthday cake," said Katie. "He said that was quite enough rent."

The two men burst into loud laughter. "Do you really expect us to believe that?" said the smaller man. "Well, whatever rent you paid you'll have to clear out. We want to be private here. We shall probably use the houseboat ourselves."

Laura began to cry. Russet growled deeply in his throat and Nick went red with anger.

"Please ring Mr Cunningham and ask him," he said. "He will tell you that he gave us permission to have this boat. We shan't interfere with you at all. We won't even come for water if you'd rather we didn't."

"You certainly won't set foot in our grounds again," said the first man roughly. "As for Mr Cunningham, he's abroad right now, as you probably very well know."

"Then ring Mrs Greyling, Laura's mother," said poor Nick, still scarlet in the face. "Mr Cunningham told her about us and the houseboat. She knows all about it. Her number is Faldham 345201."

"We'd better do that," said the first man, turning to the other. "The sooner we get these kids off the place and they understand they're not to come back, the better. Come on. We'll ring Mrs Greyling – Faldham 345201."

They went up the green lawn. The three children looked at one another, dismayed and angry. It was too bad! Mr Cunningham had said they could have the boat. But how horrible these men were! They had spoiled everything.

"I know Aunt Marion will say we're not to come here again if those men don't want us about," said Nick, with a groan. "I just know she will! Oh, why did Mr Cunningham go away? We could have phoned him and everything would have been all right. It's a great pity he didn't tell those men about us and the boat."

Meantime the men were phoning Mrs Greyling. In most polite tones the first man explained things to her. "We think there must be some mistake," he said smoothly. "We have taken over the whole property from Mr Cunningham who is, as you probably know, now away. We cannot have children using our grounds. We only took this place on Mr Cunningham's assuring us we would be completely private."

"Of course. I quite understand," said Mrs Greyling. "It's true that Mr Cunningham did say they might have the boat, but I don't want any trouble to be caused over that. I will tell the children they mustn't use it."

"Thank you, Mrs Greyling," said the smooth tones of the man. "That is kind of you. If we can make it up to the children by giving them a handsome present, we shall be glad to do so."

"No, no, of course not," said Mrs Greyling hastily. "But if you would just let them spend tonight on the boat, it would make them happy. They've carried everything there, and it would be such a disappointment if they had to come back now. I'm sure they won't do any damage."

"We will tell them they can spend tonight there, of course," said the man. "Goodnight, Mrs Greyling!" He put the receiver down, and once more went down the lawn to the houseboat. Russet growled, so the children knew he was coming. They were all afraid they might be turned out that very night.

The man hailed them. "I got on to your mother, and she agrees with me that it would be impossible to have you messing about here, now that we have taken the house. But you can stay for the night. After that, don't come near here at all. Understand?"

"Yes," said the children sulkily.

The man turned and went back up the lawn. The three children scowled after him. How they disliked him!

"I believe he's another wicked uncle!" said Katie. "He talks like the one in the shop did, with a sort of drawl."

"Well, it's no good thinking that every American we come across is Kit's wicked uncle!" said Nick. "These men can't have anything to do with him. The other man even knew Kit's name! Oh, I say, isn't it awful to think we're not to come here again?"

"I don't see why we can't," said Katie. "Why should we give up something we've every right to have just because that horrid man says we must? Let's come whenever we want to providing that man isn't here!"

"I agree," said Laura. "Just to show we don't care what he says! We know quite well that when Mr Cunningham comes back he'll say he meant us to have the boat and use it."

"I might ask the man if we could use the boat if we took it somewhere else further down the river," said Nick thoughtfully. "If we were out of his way, he wouldn't mind about the boat. We might moor it off our little island."

"Ask him tomorrow," said Katie. "What's the time, Nick? Oughtn't you to be fetching Kit? It's getting quite dark now!"

So it was. The sun had gone, and dusk was deepening.

"You girls get some supper ready, and see that the kettle is boiling," said Nick, looking at his watch. "I'll fetch Kit. Pity we haven't got better news for him!"

Nick slipped down into the boat below. The girls went into the tiny sitting-room and lit two candles. At once the cabin looked very cosy. They set up the little flap-table there and laid the supper. It looked delicious.

"Cold ham, tomatoes, fresh lettuce, bread and butter, cheese, biscuits, ripe plums, apples," said Laura. "A fine feast! I hope Nick and Kit won't be too long. Thank goodness we've got Russet with us. I'm sure he'd fly at those men if they came back again."

"I'll put the kettle on the stove," said Katie. She lit the stove in the tiny kitchen. It made a pleasant glow. Then she put the cocoa tin ready, fetched the milk, and placed a big jug beside the tin for the hot cocoa when it was made. It really was fun doing all these things on the boat!

After some time there came a shout from the dark waters. "Hi, there! Here we are! Show a light, *Black Swan*!"

Katie lit a lantern and hung it over the side to show Nick where to tie up his boat. Then the two boys clambered up on to the deck. They peered through the window of the little cabin, and looked with delight at the feast there, brightly lit by the two candles.

"What-ho for a night on board!" said Kit. "Now we're going to enjoy ourselves!"

Chapter 16

KIT GETS INTO TROUBLE

It was cosy in the little cabin, sitting squashed together round the table. All the children were very hungry, and the ham and salad soon disappeared. So did the cheese! Katie had made the cocoa, and they drank it thirstily. It was very good.

Katie and Laura cleared the supper away, washed the things, and set the table for breakfast. Then they lit candles in the tiny bedrooms, and drew the little curtains there across the windows. How small and cosy the rooms looked!

The children went into their little sleeping cabins. It was fun to undress there. Russet jumped up into Laura's bunk and curled himself round. Laura laughed.

"You'll have to move up a bit, Russet!" she said. "You're right in the very middle. Move over!"

The children snuggled into their narrow

bunks. Not one of them had ever slept in a bunk bed before, and it seemed very exciting. They pulled the bedding up round them and blew out their candles.

"Goodnight!" called the girls, and the boys answered sleepily:

"Goodnight! Sleep well!"

"Woof!" said Russet, which was his way of saying goodnight, too. He was now on Laura's feet, warm and comfortable. Everyone fell asleep at once and not one of them stirred until the morning sun put hot fingers through the cabin windows. It was nearly eight o'clock!

"Kit!" said Nick, looking in dismay at his watch. "We meant to wake at six and take you back and it's almost eight. You'll get into trouble!"

"Oh gee! I certainly will!" said Kit in horror. "We have breakfast at eight. Let's go at once! This is a disaster!"

Nick and Kit dressed hurriedly and tumbled into the little boat. "Have breakfast ready when I get back!" called Nick as the boys rowed off hurriedly. "And tell those men we shall be leaving soon if they come again."

Nick left Kit on the shore where he had picked him up the night before, then rowed back again to the houseboat. He was very hungry by the time he arrived. He smelled bacon and eggs frying, and thought it was the best smell he had ever known.

"Poor Kit!" he said as he and the two girls ate their breakfast. "I bet he really will get into awful trouble this time. I wonder what will happen."

A shout from the bank made the children look up. The two men stood there. "You're to clear off now," shouted the first man. "And remember that you're not to come here again!"

No one replied. All the children had made up their minds that they would come if they wanted to and so it wasn't a bit of good the man saying they weren't to! They washed up everything and made the deck tidy and neat.

Then they slipped down into their boat and rowed back home. It had been fun. Not as much fun as they had hoped, because those men had spoiled things, but still it had been lovely. They worried a little about Kit, and hoped he would be able to let them know how he had got on.

Nick climbed up the chestnut tree as soon as they got home, but there was no sign of anyone next door at all. He slid down, wondering if he dared to go over and find out what had happened.

"Can't you get in at the attic window without anyone seeing you?" said Laura. "Poor Kit might be locked up in his bedroom or something!"

"I'll try after lunch," said Nick. He and the others went indoors to tell Mrs Greyling all about the night on the boat. They said nothing at all about Kit, of course.

"Well, I'm afraid you mustn't go there again," she said. "The new people at the house object to children using the boat at the bottom of their garden. I do think it was rather odd of Mr Cunningham to allow you to use it when he had let the house. So I'm afraid you'll have to keep away."

Nobody said they would, and nobody said they wouldn't. They just changed the subject and told Mrs Greyling what fun they had had cooking bacon and eggs on the little stove.

After lunch Nick climbed the chestnut tree again, but still there was no sign of Kit. So the boy got under the fencing and slipped into the next-door garden. What had happened to him?

He ran silently round the grounds and up the other side to where the garage stood. The ladder was still against the wall. Kit had left it there. Up went Nick, on to the flat roof, and then into the big ash tree. Down the plank to the windowsill he slid, and in at the window. No one was there. The room was quite empty.

The boy tiptoed to the door. His heart was beating fast. He was afraid of being caught by the Dragon or by Mr Barton.

He went out on to the landing and looked over the banisters there. Below, there were three bedroom doors that he could see. Which one was Kit's?

No one seemed to be about. Nick slipped quietly down the stairs and stood in front of the bedroom doors. He opened one and peeped in. Nobody was there at all. He shut the door quietly. He tried the next.

It was locked! Was Kit locked in there? The key was on Nick's side of the door.

The boy knocked gently. There was no answer. He knocked again.

Kit's voice came: "Who is it?"

In a moment Nick had unlocked the door and was in the room. He closed the door behind him and looked round. It was Kit's bedroom! The boy was sitting huddled up before a desk, an open book in front of him. He looked very fed up and miserable.

"Nick!" said Kit, starting up and speaking in a loud whisper. "However did you get in here? The Dragon may come at any moment!"

"Can't help it," said Nick. "I just had to come and find what had happened to you!"

"The very worst," said Kit gloomily. "For some reason or other the Dragon came into my room early this morning, about five o'clock, and spotted the pillow down my bed. She woke Mr Barton, and the two hunted all over the house for me.

"Then they hunted in the garden, though they didn't see how I could be outside because all the doors and windows were securely bolted. They haven't spotted my way of escape from the attic room yet."

"What happened when you got back?" asked Nick.

"Well, I climbed up into the attic and walked down to my bedroom," said Kit, "and on the way I met the Dragon! She clutched hold of me as if she wanted to make sure I was really there. Honestly, I think she's quite fond of me!"

"Did you tell her where you had been?" asked Nick.

"Of course not, idiot!" said Kit. "She thinks I was hiding somewhere in the house to give her and Mr Barton a fright. I won't say a word and that's what has made them both so angry. I'm to be locked up in my room for two days, and do an awful lot of hard studying. I couldn't think how to get word to you but now you've come it's all right. Don't worry about me. They'll let me out the day after tomorrow but I won't be able to vanish at night any more, I'm afraid. I guess they'll keep a very sharp eye on me in future."

Suddenly the boys heard footsteps coming, and Nick felt his heart sink. He definitely didn't want to be caught just then. He looked round for a hiding place.

"Under the bed!" hissed Kit, sitting down at his desk again. "Quick!"

There was the sound of a key being jiggled in the lock, and then an exclamation as the Dragon discovered that the door was unlocked. She opened it and looked inside.

"Kit, who unlocked the door? It isn't locked and I know it was locked before. Who's been here?"

"Was the door unlocked?" said Kit, putting on a most innocent face.

"Yes it was, and it's no use trying to pretend to me!" said the Dragon, losing her temper. "Someone's been here and is here still, for all I know!"

She looked round the room and then gave a scream. She pointed to the bottom of the bed. Kit looked and, to his horror, saw that one of Nick's feet was clearly showing.

"Who's that?" cried the Dragon. "Come out, whoever you are!"

Chapter 17

PLENTY OF EXCITEMENT

Nick didn't move. He didn't know that his foot was sticking out from underneath the bed. The Dragon shouted to him again.

"Come out! If you don't, I shall drag you out!" And drag him out she did! She caught hold of his foot and pulled him roughly and strongly out from under the bed. He sat up and looked at her. "Oh! It's the boy from next door again!" she said angrily. "Didn't I tell you never to come here?"

"Yes, and you told me there wasn't a boy here," said Nick. "You told a lie!"

"How dare you come here like this?" cried the Dragon. "Oh, here is Mr Barton. He will deal with you!"

Mr Barton was a very stern-looking man who, so Kit said, never smiled at all. He looked in astonishment and anger at Nick as he was told what had happened.

"Mr Barton, I've told this boy all about

myself," said Kit. "He knows I'm in hiding, and he knows why. He wouldn't tell anyone. He's my friend."

"Your friend!" said Mr Barton scornfully, in a nasty dry voice. "You are a most foolish and irritating boy. You know quite well that we have been given instructions to keep your hiding place a secret, and to let you make no friends until that unpleasant uncle of yours is caught and dealt with. And you make things as difficult as possible for the

people who are doing their best to guard you. You deserve to be severely punished, and so does this boy, too, coming into other people's houses without permission!"

Nick felt quite frightened of Mr Barton. His eyes were so cold and piercing, and his mouth so thin-lipped and cruel.

"I'm sorry, Mr Barton," he said.

"Sorry!" said Mr Barton. "It isn't enough to be sorry. You will keep out of this house and out of the garden, too, unless you want me to complain to your parents and have you punished. Do you wish me to do that?"

"No," said Nick, who didn't want any more complaints about him to go to Mrs Greyling.

"And you will tell me exactly how you got into this house," said Mr Barton.

Nick caught a warning glance from Kit. He shut his lips tightly and did not answer.

Mr Barton lost his temper. He banged on Kit's desk, making the book jump in the air and fall to the floor.

"Do you hear me, boy?" he roared. "You will answer me!"

Nick was afraid he would have to tell. He didn't see how he could stand there for much longer and not say a word, because he was already a bit shaky at the knees. An idea came to him. No one was between him and the door. He could rush out, bang the door and slip upstairs before anyone caught him. Then he wouldn't have to say anything!

Without waiting to think about it, the boy carried out his sudden plan. He rushed to the door, banged it shut behind him, and tore up the stairs to the attic room as quickly as he could.

For a moment, Mr Barton was too astonished to do anything. Then he ran to the door and flung it open. He did not know whether Nick had gone up or down the stairs. He called to the Dragon:

"You go up to the attic and see if he is hiding there. I'll go downstairs. And if I catch him he'll regret it!"

Mr Barton ran down the stairs, and the Dragon ran up to the attic. Kit remained where he was, hoping and hoping that Nick would have time to slide out on the plank to the ash tree and get down safely.

He did! The Dragon looked into the other attic room first and then into the one that was Kit's playroom. By that time Nick was halfway down the tree. It didn't occur to the Dragon that the boy could have got out of the window, for she didn't think there was any way down to the ground. She felt sure that Nick had gone down the stairs, and she hurried down, too, to help in the search.

After about four minutes the telephone rang in the house, and Mr Barton went to answer it. It was Nick phoning from his house next door!

"Is that Mr Barton? Please don't bother to go on looking for me. I'm home. I'm sorry I can't tell you how I get in and out, and please don't be angry with Kit because I went to see him. I'll keep his secret. I promise you. I haven't told anyone at all about him."

Mr Barton was still in a furious temper. He flung down the receiver with a snort, and went to tell the Dragon.

"It beats me how those children next door get in and out! But if ever I catch one of them again, they'll be sorry!" he stormed. "As for Kit, don't let him out of your sight in future!"

The girls listened to Nick's story, holding their breath with horror when he told them how the Dragon had seen his foot sticking out from under the bed. "It was terribly exciting," said Nick, feeling quite a hero as he related the whole story.

"I think things are getting a bit too exciting!" said Katie. "And oh, Nick, I've left my dear little silver watch on the houseboat! I put it under my pillow last night and forgot to put it on my wrist again this morning! I am so sad about it, because I'm sure that nasty man will take it if he finds it."

"He certainly won't," said Nick. "I'll go and get it for you myself tomorrow. I'm not afraid of that man. I can't go today because we've got to go out with Aunt Marion. It's a good thing she's down in the village now, or I couldn't have phoned Mr Barton. It was funny to think of him and the Dragon looking upstairs and downstairs for me, and me here all the time!"

The children were sad to think of poor Kit being locked up. They didn't dare try and see him again. They went out in the car with Laura's mother to have tea with friends about ten miles away. When they came back, Nick thought about slipping away to the houseboat to fetch Katie's watch for her. But he decided not to.

"That man might be on the lookout today to see if we come back," he said. "I'll go tomorrow, after tea."

So the next day, at about five o'clock, Nick and the girls set off to walk to the river. He got into the boat and waved goodbye to them. They were going to take Russet for a nice rabbity walk. Nick rowed along, thinking of all that had been happening. He thought with dislike of Mr Barton and of the unpleasant man at the lonely house. "The Dragon's not so bad," he thought. "I'm scared of her, but I don't dislike her. Now, where's that houseboat? I should be getting near it!"

He saw the lonely house in the distance and glanced over his shoulder to see the houseboat. He couldn't seem to see it. So he stopped rowing, and twisted himself right round.

To his enormous astonishment, the boat wasn't there. It had completely disappeared!

Nick sat in his little boat, staring at the

empty space by the willow trees where the boat had always been. He wondered if he were dreaming. The houseboat had been there the day before. They had spent the night on it. And now it was gone. It was extraordinary. Nick couldn't make it out at all!

"Where has it gone?" he thought. "Can it have sunk? No, that's impossible!"

All the same Nick rowed over to the spot where the boat had been, and looked down into the deep water there. But no houseboat lay on the river bed. Only little fishes darted about by the hundred. It was most mysterious.

"Well, this beats everything!" said Nick to himself. "It really does! Whatever has happened to the *Black Swan*?"

The boy made up his mind to find it. The men must have taken it somewhere. But why? And where? It was really very odd. Nick began to row further up the river.

As he rowed, Nick watched the bank carefully. It was overgrown with weeping willow trees which were quite difficult to see through, but in one place his sharp eyes noticed that some of the branches were broken. He pulled over and found that just there, a little backwater ran into the river.

"They've taken the boat up that hidden backwater!" he thought to himself in excitement. "It'll be up there. I'll go and see."

The boy rowed under the willows and came into the little backwater. It was very pretty and very quiet. Clearly it ran alongside the grounds of the lonely house. The men must have taken the houseboat there for a reason.

"To hide it from us, I suppose!" said Nick crossly to himself. "Well, bad luck to them! I'll find it."

And find it he did! It was moored to the side, some way up the backwater, under a very big drooping willow that practically hid it. The branches hung down over the decks, and if Nick had not been looking for the boat, he might easily have passed it by, it was so well hidden!

The boy sat silently for a moment, listening for voices or sounds that might warn him of people about. But he could hear nothing. So in a second he was up on the deck and into the little cabin where

Katie had slept the night before. He slid his hand under the pillow, and felt the little silver watch. "Good!" he thought, putting it into his pocket. "Katie will be pleased. Now I'll go back and tell the girls the news."

He slipped down into his boat and rowed off again, feeling puzzled and excited. Surely the men wouldn't have taken all that trouble to hide the boat just to prevent the children from using it? And yet, what other explanation could there be? It was most extraordinary. Nick wished Mr Cunningham was home so that he could ask him a few questions.

He got back and met the girls. When he told them his news they were astonished.

"How clever of you to find the boat, Nick!" cried Katie. "And, oh, I am so glad to have my watch! I wish we could tell Kit. I hate to think of him locked up like that!"

"I'll slip in tonight, about twelve o'clock," said Nick. "Everyone next door will be asleep then. I'll give Kit a fine surprise!"

But it was Nick who got the surprise, not Kit!

Chapter 18

NICK MAKES A DISCOVERY

That night Nick set his alarm for midnight, and put the clock under his pillow. It woke him up with a jump. He was warm and sleepy and comfortable and thought that, after all, he wouldn't get out of bed and go adventuring in the middle of the night. But the sound of a car made him suddenly sit up.

The car stopped somewhere near. Nick jumped out of bed and ran over to the window. The car was parked in the drive next door. Nick could see its lights. Strange that a visitor should come at this time of the night!

"Perhaps it's Kit's tutor come back late from somewhere," thought Nick. "Well, now I'm wide awake I'll go next door after all, I think. I'll be extremely careful not to walk into the Dragon or Mr Barton, though!"

He got out of bed and slipped into his clothes. He put on his trainers and slid down the pear tree outside his window. He landed with a light thud and, in the clear moonlight, ran down the garden to the hole under the fencing.

He was by the garage in no time. The ladder was still there! Good! Up he went, and then into the dark, quiet attic. He paused at the door and listened. The house was utterly silent.

The landing was in darkness. All the doors were shut. The whole house seemed very still. Nick wondered where the late visitor was, or could it have been Mr Barton himself? He must have gone to bed very quickly then! Nick made up his mind to make no noise at all, in case Mr Barton began to wander about.

He crept down to the landing where Kit's bedroom was. He tried Kit's door. To his delight, it was not locked! The boy opened it cautiously and stepped inside.

The room looked a little different, somehow. Nick was a bit puzzled. The moonlight shone in at the window and showed everything quite clearly. Then Nick saw why it seemed different. There were two beds there, instead of one! And in each bed someone slept. Nick went cold with fear! Kit was in one bed and the Dragon was in the other! The moonlight showed up her face quite clearly. She was fast asleep.

"I suppose they've decided to have someone sleep with Kit in case he does another disappearing trick!" thought Nick. "But I daren't wake Kit in case the Dragon hears me!"

The boy tiptoed out of the room and shut the door very quietly. He heaved a sigh of relief as he stood there in the darkness.

And then he heard something that made him jump. It was a voice, coming up the stairs! It had an American drawl in it, and it was not Mr Barton's voice! Nick stood there, wondering whether he dared slip up the stairs to the attic. He couldn't see who was coming, for a bend of the stairs hid the two men. Then, with a sigh of relief, he heard them go into a little room on the half-landing below.

"What an odd time for someone to come and talk to Mr Barton!" thought Nick. "I do hope he isn't going to send Kit away, now he's aware that I know his secret. That would be too bad."

The boy tiptoed down the stairs a little way, wondering if he could hear whether Kit was to be sent away or not; and what he did hear sent a shock of horror down his back!

"You can have ten thousand pounds as soon as the boy is in our hands," said the American voice. "No more, and that's flat!"

Nick could not move. What did this mean? Why should Mr Barton have ten thousand pounds? And was Kit the boy they spoke of? If so, that meant that Mr Barton was a traitor. He was bargaining with Kit's enemies. Perhaps Kit's wicked uncle was the man in that little room!

"Come here tomorrow night and I'll hand him over," said Mr Barton's voice. "Bring the money with you in cash. You can't have him tonight. That woman insisted on sleeping with him. Have you got a safe place to put him in? There's sure to be a great uproar if he disappears. I'll have to tell the police and pretend all kinds of things."

"We've got a fine place," said the other

man. "No one would ever look there. Have him ready as soon as it's dark tomorrow. Bring him in the car to that spot we arranged, and I'll take him from there. If you play your part well, no one will ever know you had anything to do with it. It's up to you!"

The door was opened and the two men came out. Nick darted up the stairs a little way. He wished he could have seen the

other man. He was convinced that it must be the man who had questioned him in the ice-cream shop. The wicked uncle! Somehow he must have found out where Kit was, after all!

He heard the men go downstairs. He heard the front door open and a car door slam. He heard the roar of the engine being started up and then the car was gone! Mr Barton came indoors and locked and bolted the door. Nick fled upstairs to the attic. He slid down the tree and was back in his own garden in record time. He was trembling. Things were becoming very serious. He wondered what he had better do.

Somehow or other he had to warn Kit, that was obvious. Should he tell Aunt Marion? No, she wouldn't believe such a tale, and might go straight to Mr Barton, and then he would be warned. Should they tell the Dragon? No! She might perhaps be a traitor, too. Nick couldn't tell if she was or not. Poor Kit! It was terrible to be in someone's power like that, and to be handed over to a wicked man.

The boy went into the girls' room and woke them. He poured out his tale in whispers. They were horrified. Laura began to cry. "Let's tell Mum," she sobbed. "I don't want Kit to be kidnapped. Please let's tell Mum."

"No," said Nick. "I've got a much better idea. *We'll* kidnap Kit and hide him! We'll keep him safe till we can think what's the best thing to do. We can't make plans in a hurry."

"But where can we hide him? Here, in the house?" said Katie, astonished. "Aunt Marion would soon find out."

"Of course not here," said Nick scornfully. "I've got a much better place than that. We'll hide him on the *Black Swan*!"

"On the houseboat!" echoed the girls. "Of course! What a brilliant idea!"

"Nobody would ever think of looking for him there," said Nick. "We'd be the only people who would know. We could take him food each day. His enemies would never think of looking in a place they've not even heard of!"

"That's exactly what we'll do!" said Katie. "Kit will be quite safe there. When shall we take him?"

"We must take him as soon as possible tomorrow," said Nick. "We need to hurry. Mr Barton is supposed to hand him over in the evening. What a nasty man he is!"

"I never did like the look of him," said Laura.

"Nor did I," said Katie. "O-o-oh! This is getting very exciting! I feel as if I must be in a dream!"

"Well, you'd better go to sleep again now," said Nick, getting off the bed. "We have work to do tomorrow!"

They all fell asleep after a time, and when they woke in the morning they could hardly believe that it was all true!

Nick climbed up the chestnut tree to see if Kit was by any chance on the lawn below. He was, but the Dragon and Mr Barton were there as well.

Kit glanced up at the top of the chestnut tree. He was longing to get a glimpse of the children. Nick waggled a branch wildly, and Kit felt certain someone was there. He picked up a ball and began to throw it idly. Nick slid down the tree again.

"He's seen me, I'm sure," he said. "He picked up his ball and I think it was a signal to me to throw him over a message. I'll write one now. You find the old split ball."

Soon the message was crammed inside the ball, and Nick threw it over into the next door garden. Kit was on the watch for it. Neither the Dragon nor Mr Barton noticed the second ball dropping on to the lawn. They merely thought it was the one that Kit was playing with. The boy picked it up and went behind the summerhouse. He read the short message:

Kit –
You are in great danger. Go to the tunnel as soon as you can. We'll be there.
        Nick, Katie and Laura

Kit put the note into his pocket. He threw his ball high into the air, and it fell with a crash into the bushes beyond. Kit made as if to go and get it.

"You're not to go out of sight, Kit," said Mr Barton sharply.

"I'm only just going to get my ball, Mr Barton," said Kit meekly, and went into the bushes. He ran rapidly down the garden as soon as he was out of sight and came to the hole. The others were there, on the other side. In a few words Nick told the surprised boy all about the happenings of the night before, and how he had found out that Mr Barton was a traitor ready to hand Kit over to the kidnappers that night.

"We're going to hide you on the *Black Swan*," whispered Nick. "Can you come now, this very minute? Oh, no, there's Mr Barton yelling for you. He'll be along in a moment. Escape into our garden the first chance you have, and go down to our boat by the river. We'll come there with food as soon as we can."

Kit's eyes nearly fell out of his head as he heard all that Nick had to tell him. He went back to meet the angry Mr Barton, planning how to escape down to the boat the first minute he could.

"What luck we've got such a good hiding place for me," he thought. "No one in the world would ever think of hunting for me there!"

Chapter 19

KIT TRIES TO ESCAPE

Kit had to go back to Mr Barton, who was very angry indeed with him for going off.

"Didn't I forbid you to go out of my sight?" he shouted, and actually gave the boy a cuff, a thing he had never done before. The Dragon spoke up at once, much to Kit's surprise.

"Don't hit Kit! You know you've no right to do that!"

"Hold your tongue," growled Mr Barton. "This boy has to learn to do what he is told. How can we keep him in hiding and look after him if he disappears whenever he wants to?"

"I don't think you ought to hit him," said the Dragon in an obstinate tone. "The boy doesn't have much fun. Let him alone."

Kit felt grateful to the Dragon for sticking up for him. He went to her and picked up her knitting wool, which had slipped off her lap and fallen to the ground.

"Thank you, Dragon!" he said in a low voice. Miss Taylor looked a little less fierce, and her eyes gave the boy a kindly glance. Mr Barton sat down again in his chair, muttering something.

"Don't anger him," said the Dragon. "He's in a funny mood today."

Kit sat quietly beside the Dragon, pretending to read a book. He worried about what Nick had told him. He simply must escape as soon as he could. He had plenty of courage, but the thought of being kidnapped and held prisoner in some unpleasant place once again filled him with horror. He wished he had a father and mother as most children had. He had nobody but his wicked uncle and a great-aunt who had put him in the care of the Dragon and Mr Barton.

"All I've got to do is to run down the garden and escape under the fencing," he kept telling himself. "I wish it didn't take so long scrabbling through that hole. Mr Barton would discover me long before I could get through. How and when shall I escape?"

Kit tried two or three times to give Mr Barton the slip that day. When he went to wash his hands for lunch, he turned into the kitchen instead of into the cloakroom, hoping to be able to slip out through the door before anyone noticed him.

But Mr Barton had followed him down the hallway and into the kitchen! He ordered him out at once.

"What are you doing here? I sent you to wash your hands, not come in here! Go at once and do what you are told!"

Kit meekly washed his hands and took his place at the table. He wondered if he could get permission to go up to his attic playroom after lunch, then he could escape down the tree. So he asked Mr Barton.

"May I set out my railway this afternoon in the attic?" he asked.

"No. You are going to study with me out in the summerhouse," said his tutor, who was quite determined not to let Kit out of his sight once that day.

So poor Kit had to sit in the summerhouse and learn some French until teatime. Then Mr Barton took him firmly by the arm and led him indoors.

It was the same after tea. Mr Barton kept Kit close beside him, and the boy began to despair. "Could I take a run round the garden, sir?" he asked at last.

"Yes," said Mr Barton, and Kit got up joyfully. Now was his chance. But his heart sank as Mr Barton rose, too.

"I will come with you," he said. And he went with Kit all the way round the grounds. Kit did not go near the hole under the fencing! He was not going to give Mr Barton the chance of discovering that!

"I don't think you need sleep in Kit's room tonight, Miss Taylor," Mr Barton said to the Dragon at suppertime. "That room is really too small for two people."

"I think I would rather sleep with him," said the Dragon.

"I have had your bed taken out of Kit's room," said Mr Barton. "I will see him into bed myself and then lock the door. He will be quite safe."

The Dragon said no more, but she was angry. She had never liked the surly Mr Barton, and now she liked him even less. Kit looked and felt miserable. How in the world could he escape if Mr Barton did things like that? If he was locked into his room he couldn't possibly get out. There was a sheer drop to the ground from his bedroom window. He would break his neck if he tried to escape that way.

"Mr Barton wants to make sure I'm under lock and key when darkness comes, so that he can hand me over," thought the boy desperately. "Whatever am I to do?"

There really did seem nothing he could do at all, as long as his tutor kept him under his eye. It was no good running off. Mr Barton was on the watch for any tricks. The boy sat down with a book, trying to plan something.

"You had better go to bed early tonight, Kit," said Mr Barton, in smooth tones. "You look tired. Come along upstairs now."

"I'm not tired," said Kit indignantly. "It's only a quarter to eight!"

But he had to go. Mr Barton took hold of his arm and held it firmly. Kit found himself in his bedroom and had to undress.

"Get into bed," ordered Mr Barton, and into bed poor Kit got. Then Mr Barton said goodnight and went out of the room. He locked the door behind him and took the key out of the lock. Now even the Dragon could not get in.

Kit got up and dressed. He put his pyjamas on over his clothes, in case Mr Barton suddenly came back. He knew now that his only chance of escape was to slip quickly out of the door when Mr Barton opened it later on to take him away.

"And sure thing, he'll say that somebody is after me, and I've got to go away with him and hide!" thought the boy. "That would be his way of getting me to my wicked uncle! Well, I'll take the bulb out of the light so that when Mr Barton turns on the switch it won't light! That'll give me a chance to escape."

He took the bulb out of the lamp. Then he settled down on a chair behind the door, waiting for Mr Barton.

About nine o'clock he heard him coming and stood up, his heart beating fast. Now he must take his chance, for he wouldn't have another!

Mr Barton put the key in the door and unlocked it. He opened the door and put his hand out to turn on the switch for the light. Click went the switch, but there was no light! The room remained in darkness.

Mr Barton gave an annoyed hiss and went into the room to turn on the light beside Kit's bed. Kit took his chance! In a second he was round the door and up the stairs to the attic.

Mr Barton heard him and saw him go round the door, as he had left on the light in the passage outside. He gave a shout and was after the boy at once.

Kit knew it would be no good trying to escape out of the attic window with Mr Barton so close behind him. He wouldn't have time even to slide across the plank to the tree. He must try and hide somewhere for a few minutes and then, when he saw his chance, he could try the attic window. So, quick as lightning, the boy stood on a chair beside a cupboard and then, with a deft leap, he was on the top of the cupboard. Very cautiously, he lay down flat. It was a big cupboard and tall.

Mr Barton rushed on to the landing and up the stairs. He passed by the cupboard and went straight into Kit's playroom. No one was there!

The man was in a real fury. "Kit, you

will be severely punished for behaving like this! What do you think you're doing? These silly ways you have of hiding have got to stop! Come out at once!"

Kit lay on top of the cupboard and made no sound at all. Mr Barton went on and on talking, trying to get Kit to come out, and his voice became more and more angry.

Then Kit heard a car driving up outside, and he guessed it was his wicked uncle come to find out why Mr Barton hadn't handed him over at the time and place arranged. His heart began to beat so fast that he was afraid Mr Barton would hear it!

Mr Barton heard the car, too. He didn't dare to go down and answer the door, because he was afraid that Kit would give him the slip if he did. So he called down to the Dragon.

"Miss Taylor, open the door and bring my visitor up here, please!"

In a minute or two the visitor came upstairs. "What's up?" he asked in a low tone. "Where's the kid?"

"I was just going to bring him along when he dashed out of his bedroom and upstairs here somewhere," said Mr Barton in an angry voice. "Wait till I catch him! I'll box his ears and give him the best hiding he's ever had in his life!"

Kit lay still on the top of the cupboard. He felt certain he would be discovered sooner or later. Then an idea came to him. He had his ball in his pocket. Suppose he took it and threw it hard into the boxroom opposite him! It would make a noise in there, and the men would be sure to think it was him! If they rushed into the boxroom he could slip down from the cupboard, run to his playroom and escape!

Kit took his ball quietly from his pocket and then, with a violent jerk of his arm, threw it with all his might into the little boxroom opposite the cupboard. It made a great noise there, bouncing and rolling about, and the two men at once thought that the boy was in the boxroom. They rushed into the room, switched on the light and shut the door so that the boy could not run out of it if he was there!

This was just what Kit wanted! He slipped down from the cupboard and ran to the playroom. He shut the door and turned the key in the lock. The two men would have a job getting in, which would give him a chance to escape!

The men saw at a glance that the boxroom hid no boy, and when they heard the sound of Kit going to the attic room, they rushed over to it just in time to see the door close and to hear the key turned!

They hammered on the door. "You bad boy!" yelled Mr Barton. "Open this door at once!"

Kit ran to the window. Mr Barton put his shoulder to the door and heaved hard. The door began to splinter, for it wasn't strong. In a moment it would break! Kit slid across the plank, trembling.

"I can do it!" he said to himself. "I can do it! Come on, Kit, don't get caught!"

Chapter 20

AN EXCITING NIGHT

The door of the playroom fell in with a crash, for both men had thrown their weight and strength against it. Kit heard the crash as he slithered down the ash tree. He was so excited that he almost lost his hold and fell, but just managed to save himself in time.

Mr Barton had run to the window, and at once saw the plank reaching across to the ash tree, illuminated by the playroom light.

"Look at that!" he cried. "This is how the boy has escaped from the house whenever he wanted to, and how that boy next door came in! Let's go downstairs quickly and catch him in the garden."

Both men tore down the stairs, but by this time Kit was on the ground and speeding as fast as he could down the garden to the hole under the fencing. The men saw his dark shadow and went after him. Mr Barton had a torch which he trained on Kit.

The boy plunged into some thick undergrowth and then made his way quietly to the hole under the fencing. The men plunged about in the undergrowth, trying their best to find the boy.

Kit lay on his tummy and began to slide beneath the fencing, down the curving passage the children had made. He was almost through when the two men came up, panting and Mr Barton saw the curious passage by the light of his torch. He was almost speechless with rage.

"Look at that!" he cried. "Those children next door must have done this. This is how they've been getting in and out of the garden, and that nasty dog, too! Kit, how dare you behave like this? Come back at once!"

But Kit didn't. He tore off into the darkness, leaving the two men standing there, helpless, for they were both too big to wriggle through that hole. It was only large enough to take children and dogs!

Kit wondered what to do. Would it be any good going down to the boat now it was dark? The children would not be there. He decided to go quietly to the house and see if there was a light in Nick's bedroom.

There was! A shower of small stones brought Nick to the window at once. In a moment he was down the pear tree and standing eagerly beside Kit.

"We'd almost given you up, and were wondering whether to tell Aunt Marion or the police," said Nick. "We've got all the food into the boat. Come down now and I'll row you to the houseboat and you can tell me what's happened. We must go while it's dark."

The two boys hurried down to the boat. They got in and Nick took the oars. Kit told him all that had happened, and Nick listened in growing excitement. Kit had only just escaped in time!

"I think you've been extremely clever," said Nick admiringly. "I really do. Throwing that ball to make a noise in the boxroom was a brilliant idea. How angry those two men must have been when they saw you wriggling through our tunnel and couldn't get through it themselves."

Nick came to the little backwater and slid the boat up it. When he had gone some way up, he shone a torch towards the trees and Kit caught sight of the houseboat.

"Hey! It's really well hidden, isn't it?" he said. "I bet no one will ever find me here!"

They rowed to the *Black Swan* and climbed up on its deck. Then they went down into one of the little sleeping cabins.

They looked round the cabin in surprise. It wasn't as they had left it. Someone had made up a bed on one of the bunks and put food and water on the little chest.

"I suppose one of the men from the house must have slept here yesterday," said

Nick, puzzled. "It's a good thing he's not here tonight! Shall I open a window, Kit? It feels awfully hot with the window closed."

"I'll open it," said Kit, and tried to push the little window, but it wouldn't move. He went outside and shone a torch on it. He saw that a nail had been inserted so that the window couldn't be opened from the inside. "I don't know what those men have been doing here," he said. "They must be afraid of burglars if they've nailed up the windows."

"I'll have to go now, Kit," said Nick. "I hope you won't feel too lonely here on your own. And no one will come along tonight, it's too late. Anyway, if you hear anyone, just slip off the boat and hide in a willow tree. The branches come down low over the ground."

"Right!" said Kit. "Thanks for all you've done, Nick. Come again tomorrow and we'll decide what to do. I'm out of Mr Barton's clutches for the time being anyway!"

Nick slid down the side of the houseboat and got into his own little boat. He called a low goodbye to Kit and rowed away down the quiet backwater to the river.

Kit threw himself on the bunk fully dressed, and then saw that he still had his clothes on under his pyjamas! "I'll be too hot!" he thought, and took them off. Then he lay down again, feeling tired out with excitement. His eyes shut and very soon he was fast asleep.

Nick rowed back quickly, longing to tell Katie and Laura what had happened. He tied up the boat and made his way across the fields, letting himself in at the gate at the bottom of the garden.

Suddenly he heard sounds nearby! He flattened himself against a tree and listened breathlessly. He saw the torchlight being flashed around, and guessed that Mr Barton and the wicked uncle had found their way into the garden and were searching for Kit, thinking he might be hiding there.

He stayed behind the tree, listening to the low voices of the men and watching the flashing of torches. He wondered what the men would do when they didn't find Kit. No way would they get a word out of the two girls or Nick! Nick began to wonder what Kit himself ought to do. It rather looked as if they'd have to talk to Aunt

Marion soon. He decided to tell her in the morning.

Suddenly, as Nick stood behind the tree, he felt something cold pressed against his bare leg, and he jumped violently. Then he gave a sigh of relief! It was only Russet putting his nose against Nick's calf. He had come to find Nick, and had actually not barked or growled at the two men. Russet was most remarkable, the way he knew when to keep quiet!

Nick decided it was time to get back to the house. He felt tired, and it really seemed as if the two men meant to spend the whole night hunting in the garden! So, cautiously, he made his way towards a little path a good way off from where the men were searching. But Russet didn't move so cautiously, and made a noise in the undergrowth!

At once the men called to one another:

"What's that? Is that the boy? Over there, quick!"

Nick slipped behind another tree. Russet discovered a rabbit-hole and put his nose down it. As Nick didn't seem to mind the men, he did not mind them either. Russet smelled rabbit so strongly that he got very excited. He scrabbled at the hole with his front paws and sent a whole lot of earth flying into the air. It pattered to the ground, making a slight noise.

The men darted over to the sound at once, and got a shower of small stones and earth all over them. Nick chuckled quietly. Good old Russet! The boy slipped away as the men came near, and ran quietly down the path to the house. He could escape nicely while the men were trying to locate Russet!

"Why, it's only a dog!" said Mr Barton in disgust as his torch showed up Russet's back legs. His front ones were in the hole, with his head. "That wretched dog again! He's always appearing. Come on, we can't find the boy now. He's gone into hiding somewhere, but he won't feel quite so cheerful in the morning after a night in the open, and no breakfast to look forward to! He'll probably come creeping back to the house, and we'll get him then. I'll pay him back for leading us a dance like this!"

"And so will I," said the other man grimly. They went quietly out of the garden and into the gates of their own house. Nick heard the front door slam as he leaned out of his window.

The girls came creeping into his room. They hadn't been able to sleep because they had been so worried about Kit. Nick grinned at them.

"It's all right," he said. "Kit had a frightfully narrow escape, but he's safe on the houseboat now. When I came up the garden, I nearly ran into Mr Barton and the wicked uncle hunting all over the place for him! Russet scrabbled earth over them from a rabbit-hole."

"Oh, Nick, what do we do next?" asked Katie.

"We'll wait till tomorrow before we do anything more," said Nick, yawning. "I'm going to sleep. Goodnight!"

And what a to-do there was in the morning.

Chapter 21

A Very Strange Thing

The next morning the Dragon was astonished not to see Kit at breakfast. She ate her cereal and said nothing for a few minutes, expecting Kit to come. Then she spoke to Mr Barton, who was reading the newspaper, looking surly and stern.

"Why isn't Kit down?" she asked.

"He's having breakfast in bed," said Mr Barton. This was a lie, of course. Kit was far away on the houseboat!

"Why? Is he ill?" asked the Dragon.

"No," said Mr Barton shortly.

"I shall go up and see him," said the Dragon, and she rose.

"Sit down," said Mr Barton, beginning to lose his temper again. "I'm in charge of this boy."

"I am too," said the Dragon, and she began to look fierce.

"You're only supposed to see to his

clothes, food and health," said Mr Barton. "If you interfere with me, I shall have you discharged."

The Dragon rose from the table and, before Mr Barton could stop her, she was out of the door and up the stairs. She came to Kit's door. It was shut and locked! The key had been taken away. The Dragon frowned. She didn't like all this locking up.

She knocked on the door. "Kit! Have you got your breakfast? Are you all right?"

There was no answer, which was not surprising, considering that the room was empty. The Dragon knocked again. As there was still no answer, she began to look worried.

"Kit! Are you there? Answer me!"

But there was no reply at all. The Dragon went downstairs and faced Mr Barton.

"I don't believe Kit is there! There isn't any reply when I knock on the door. I demand that you open the door, Mr Barton! If you don't, I shall go to the police."

Mr Barton was feeling worried himself, but about his ten thousand pounds, not Kit! If the boy didn't turn up he would lose the money, and it really did seem as if the boy had escaped. Though why he should run away, Mr Barton couldn't think. He didn't know that Kit had been warned against him.

The Dragon rapped angrily on the table. "Mr Barton! Do you hear me? Unless you open Kit's door at once, I shall ring the police!"

There was nothing for it but to open the door. The Dragon would certainly do what she said, and then Mr Barton might get into trouble. He would open the door and then pretend to be most astonished that Kit wasn't there. He would try to persuade the Dragon that Kit was playing another of his tricks and would soon be back.

So he got up from the table, took the bedroom key from his pocket and went upstairs with the Dragon. "He is probably feeling in a sulky mood and won't answer you," he said as he fitted the key in the door. He opened the door and the Dragon gave a cry.

"He's not here! His bed is empty! What's happened to Kit? Mr Barton, do you know anything about this?"

Mr Barton was doing his very best to seem as astonished as the Dragon. He opened his eyes wide and looked all round the room in surprise, as if he expected Kit to be hiding behind the door or a chest of drawers.

"Now where can he be?" he said.

"Mr Barton, has Kit been kidnapped again?" cried the Dragon, looking rather white. "How could he have disappeared out of this room when the door was locked? He couldn't possibly have jumped out of that window. He'd have broken his neck!"

"Ah, but someone might have come in at the window and taken him!" said Mr Barton. "Now don't let's worry for a little while, Miss Taylor. The boy may possibly have slipped out of the room before I locked the door, and be hiding from us. You know how full of silly tricks he is."

The Dragon stared at Mr Barton, hardly believing a word he said. "What was all that running about and shouting I heard last night?" she asked suddenly. "Just after I sent that visitor upstairs to you?"

"Running and shouting?" said Mr Barton in an innocent voice. "I don't know.

You must have been mistaken. Now let's go downstairs and finish our breakfast in peace. Kit will probably turn up before we have finished."

"Well, if he hasn't, I'll ring the police at once!" said the Dragon, and she sounded as if she was almost in tears! She was fond of Kit in spite of her fierceness.

They sat down and finished breakfast. Mr Barton felt furious with the Dragon for interfering, and he quickly made plans. If she wanted to ring the police, he certainly couldn't stop her. He must pretend to be as upset and puzzled as the Dragon herself. No one could suspect him of kidnapping the boy.

"The police will soon find Kit, wherever he is hiding," he thought, "and then they'll bring him back to me, of course. That'll be my chance to hand him over to his uncle straight away. So I'll get my ten thousand pounds after all. Yes, I think on the whole I shan't do too badly if I do let Miss Taylor ring the police. She'll begin to think there is something strange about my behaviour if I try to stop her."

So when the Dragon went to the

telephone and asked for the police, Mr Barton said nothing to prevent her. He spoke to the police himself, and told them how Kit had been kidnapped twice before in America.

"But this time I am sure the boy has not been kidnapped," said Mr Barton in his smoothest tones. "I feel certain he has run away, as a boyish escapade. Naturally it annoyed him to have to be kept in hiding almost like a prisoner. If you could find him for us it would be a great relief."

A police inspector was round at the house in half an hour, questioning the Dragon and Mr Barton. He seemed to agree with Mr Barton that Kit had only run away for a prank.

"Boys will be boys!" said the inspector. "Leave it to me. We'll let you know as soon as we hear of any stray boy in the district. Anyway, he'll probably come back of his own accord as soon as he feels hungry."

"Quite likely," agreed Mr Barton. The tutor wished he could get hold of Nick and question him about Kit. He felt sure that the children next door had much more to do with Kit than he had realised. That hole under the fencing must have been used very often by one or all of them.

When the police inspector had gone, the telephone rang. Mr Barton went to answer it. He heard the cautious voice of Kit's uncle speaking.

"Any news?"

"None," said Mr Barton, "except that Miss Taylor called the police in. But if they find the boy they're going to hand him over to me and you can come and get him at once."

"No," said the voice. "I'm not risking being caught through coming over to your house. I'll show you the hiding place I've prepared for him, and you can take him there yourself. Meet me the other side of Faldham in half an hour."

"Where's this wonderful hiding place?" asked Mr Barton impatiently. "You're always talking about it."

There was pause. "It's a houseboat!" was the reply. "You know we took that lonely house on the river? Well, we found there was a houseboat that went with the property. Some children were playing on it, but we turned them off. We towed it up into a little backwater near the house, and hid it under some willows. We've got it all ready for the boy. Nobody in the world would guess he was there. We've nailed up the windows and have got a padlock for the door, so that he can't possibly get away."

Mr Barton gave a long whistle. "A very good place," he said. "All right, I'll meet you outside Faldham in half an hour and you can show it to me. Then, when I get the boy again, I'll take him straight to the boat so that he won't be seen going to your house. I can take him there by going up the river, can't I?"

"That's the idea," said Kit's uncle. "If you take him at night, no one will see you. We'll look after him then!"

"And what about my money?" asked Mr Barton.

"You don't get a penny until the boy is delivered to us," was the answer. "As soon as that boy is on board the boat, you'll have your reward."

Mr Barton put down the telephone and went to get the car out. He would see exactly where this wonderful hiding place was, and then take Kit there just as soon as he could lay hands on him again!

But of course, Kit was there already! He was actually hiding himself in the very hiding place that the kidnappers had themselves got ready for him, but he didn't know it. And they in turn didn't know that Kit was there! This was surely one of the strangest things that could possibly happen!

Now Mr Barton was on the way to see this hiding place, and Kit was there. Look out, Kit, you're in danger again!

Chapter 22

A Narrow Escape

That morning Nick decided to go and talk things over with Kit before he told Aunt Marion anything about all the exciting happenings of the day before. So he took his boat and rowed off up the river. He passed the little island, went by the lonely house, and slid up the hidden backwater. He came to the *Black Swan* and cautiously tied his boat on the farther side of it, under a bush so that it could not be seen.

Then he clambered on to the bank and went to the weeping willows that hid the big houseboat. He stood there for a moment, listening. He could hear nothing. He stepped on to the deck of the houseboat and made his way to the cabin where Kit had slept the night before.

Kit was there, reading a book. He didn't hear Nick because he was so quiet, and he jumped violently when he heard his voice saying, "Kit! Is everything all right?"

"Hey! You made me jump almost out of my skin!" cried Kit. "It's great to see you! I had a very good night and slept like a log. I couldn't think where in the world I was when I woke up this morning!"

Nick grinned. "You didn't worry much about enemies, then," he said. "The girls and I hardly slept a wink for worrying about you. Listen, Kit, I want to discuss with you what's the best thing to do now. Shall we tell Aunt Marion? I have a feeling she might not believe us and Uncle Peter is still away on business. If Mr Barton is very clever and tells Aunt Marion a whole lot of believable lies, it'll be very difficult for us to stop you being handed over to him again."

"Yes," said Kit thoughtfully. "Perhaps it would be best to wait a bit. But, Nick, I really do believe you'd be safe to tell the Dragon. I think she's fond of me, and I know she hates Mr Barton. Couldn't you just go and see her and find out if she's upset about my disappearing? If she is, then tell her what you know and then, if ever I'm captured by Mr Barton again, she won't let him have charge of me."

"She's such a fierce person," said Nick, not at all liking the idea of talking to the Dragon by himself.

"She looks as fierce as twenty dragons, I know," agreed Kit. "But she's not really. I wish I knew for certain whether she's my friend or my enemy. I don't see how we're to know!"

But they did know, and in a very short time, too!

Suddenly they heard the sound of voices from the bank, and the two boys in the sleeping cabin sat up straight in alarm. Kit's uncle was about to show Mr Barton the hiding place he had prepared for Kit once he had been kidnapped. Little did they know that the boy was already there!

"It's somebody coming!" whispered Nick.

"Get into the little hanging cupboard, quick!" said Kit. "Look, behind that curtain there, where people hang their coats. I'll hide behind the one in the next cabin."

There was a door between the two sleeping cabins, and Kit was soon in the next one, hiding behind the curtain. He heard the footsteps of the men as they came on board the houseboat.

They stood on the deck, talking. Kit peeped out from behind the curtain and caught a glimpse of them through the nailed-up windows. His heart went cold and his knees began to shake.

One of the men was Mr Barton – and the other must be his wicked uncle! Kit was as sure of it as he could be. He had never seen his uncle, but there was a distinct family resemblance in that cruel face, with its cold blue eyes and thin-lipped mouth. The voice had an American drawl, too.

"Well, Mr Barton, what do you think of the hiding place we've got for my nephew?" said the American voice. "Right away from anywhere, isn't it?"

"Yes, it's a good place," said Mr Barton. "How do I get to it from the river? Let's see, I could get a boat where the river bends round not far from the bottom of our garden, row straight up, and then look out for this backwater."

"You'll know where the backwater is because it's not far past the house," said

Kit's uncle. "It's the only house on the bank for miles, so you can't mistake it. Come down into the cabins and you'll see the boy will be quite comfortable, if a little lonely! We've had the windows nailed up and I've got a padlock for the door – here it is, on the window ledge – and I had to get a new door, because the old one was very rotten. He can't possibly escape once we get him here."

To the horror of the two hidden boys the men walked into the little sleeping cabins. Kit tried to think whether he had left anything out. The food was in the kitchen under the table. They might not see that. But he had left his book out and he thought his pyjamas must be over the chair, where he had thrown them the night before.

The men looked round the cabins. They had no idea at all that the boy they were hunting for was at that very moment within a metre of them, behind a curtain either of them could have touched!

Kit and Nick were trembling from head to foot. Now they realised that the hiding place they had chosen for Kit was the same one that the enemy had also prepared for him. Now they knew why the windows had been nailed up! Now they knew why the sleeping cabin had been prepared for someone and why food and drink had been put ready on the chest. It was all for Kit, who should have been handed over to the enemy the night before, and brought to the boat as a prisoner!

And by a very strange chance, the children had chosen the same hiding place for Kit, under the nose of the enemy. Could anything be stranger or more frightening?

Both boys felt quite certain that at any moment the curtains would be pulled aside and they would be discovered. Kit hoped desperately that he wouldn't cough or sneeze. He felt sure a sneeze was coming.

"I wish we knew where that wretched boy was," said Mr Barton angrily. "I had him all locked up, and was just going to get him when he sprang out of the door past me. He must be hiding in the countryside somewhere now. But the police are looking for him, so he should be found soon."

This was news to the boys.

"It's a pity you couldn't stop that interfering Miss Taylor from getting in the police," said Kit's uncle irritably. "I suppose we couldn't buy her help, could we? Would she stop bothering about the boy, and go away and leave us a free hand, if we gave her a few thousand pounds?"

"No, I'm certain she wouldn't," said Mr Barton at once. "She's fond of the boy – goodness knows why. She has a funny way of showing it, for she's a sulky kind of woman, but I don't think you could get her on your side. She knew the boy's father very well, and went to the boy at once when she heard of the plane crash."

"Well, we can't count on her help, then," said Kit's uncle. "I'll tell you what we'll do: we'll send her the ransom notes when we've got the boy. We'll say that we'll set Kit free on payment of a large sum of money, and she must be the go-between. If she hands over the money from the boy's great-aunt, who's in charge of his fortune, we'll hand over the boy! I shan't appear in this at all, of course. I've plenty of go-betweens who can't possibly be traced back to me. All you've got to do is to keep your mouth shut, take your money and quietly disappear when we get hold of the boy."

"I know that," said Mr Barton. "If only I could find him!"

He could have if he had just stretched out his left hand! The boys behind the curtain listened to every word, and Kit felt furious when he heard what a traitor Mr Barton had turned out to be. But he was glad to know that the Dragon was on his side, and not on his uncle's. That was something to be thankful for.

"Well, come on!" said Mr Barton at last. "I've had enough of this stuffy cabin. I know my way here all right, and when I get hold of the boy, I'll bring him here, lock him up, and then go back and phone you. I'll simply say that 'the parcel has arrived'. You'll know what I mean."

Kit's uncle laughed. "Yes, I'll know," he said. "Now, come up to the house and have a drink before you go."

To the great relief of the boys, the men left the houseboat and made their way back to the house. They hadn't noticed either book or pyjamas after all! Kit darted out from the cabin and peered between the willows to make sure they had gone. Then he went back to Nick.

"Hey! To think that I came to the very hiding place that was prepared for me!" said Kit at last.

"You'd better stay here," said Nick. "After all, it's the last place your uncle would expect to find you. You've got plenty of food. I'll get straight back now and tell the Dragon everything. Then she can go and tell Aunt Marion and between them they'll know what to do. You keep safe here till I come and tell you what's been decided."

"Okay," said Kit. "Hey, when those men know we were just under their noses in these cabins, won't they be furious!"

Chapter 23

A Marvellous Surprise

Nick slipped into his little boat and began to row down the backwater as quickly as he could. He wanted to tell the adults the whole story now. It seemed suddenly to have grown very serious. Before, it had been rather fun and very exciting, but since Nick had stood trembling behind the curtain, within reach of two kidnappers, he hadn't felt it was amusing at all!

"It's getting nasty!" he thought as he rowed strongly back down the river. "We've got to do something now. I'll go in and see the Dragon as soon as I get back!"

First of all he went to tell Katie and Laura the latest news. They could hardly believe it!

"Oh, let's tell Mum, quick!" said Laura. "I'm frightened."

"You've forgotten your mother's out for the day," said Katie. "We'd better go next door and tell the Dragon. Come on, let's do it now!"

"Wait, Mr Barton may be back," said Nick, who didn't want to run the risk of running into that unpleasant man. "I'll go and see if his car's in the drive first."

It was. So he was back already! This was a blow. Nick climbed up the chestnut tree to see if the Dragon was on the lawn by herself. If so, they might perhaps squeeze through the hole and go and call her. So up the tree he went, and came down again, beaming.

"Yes, she's there, reading, and Mr Barton isn't anywhere to be seen. Come on, we'll go through the hole."

So down the garden they went to the hole under the fencing. But to their anger and dismay somebody had filled the whole thing in! They could no longer use it. They stood there, red with rage.

"Oh no!" said Nick angrily. "Mr Barton must have done this! Now what are we to do? I really don't feel like going and knocking at the front door!"

"We'd better watch until Mr Barton goes out again, if he does go out," said Katie.

"I'll take first watch, over there, in the hedge."

"Right," said Nick. "We'll take turns of half an hour each. Then as soon as he goes out we'll pop in and tell the Dragon everything."

So Laura took the first watch, and after half an hour Nick came to take his turn, and then Katie. After lunch they watched again, and got very tired of it. Teatime and still Mr Barton didn't go out. The children began to despair.

And then, about half past six, Nick who was on watch, saw, to his great delight, the figure of Mr Barton going down the drive. He was going to the post, for he had a letter in his hand. Good! Now was their chance!

Nick gave a low whistle, and the others came running up. Russet was with them.

"He's gone out!" said Nick. "Come on! It's the only chance we'll have. We'll take Russet with us, because I shall feel a bit safer if we have a dog to guard us."

The children walked up the drive to the house next door. They rang the bell. The housekeeper opened the door. "Please can we speak to Miss Taylor?" said Nick.

"Well," said the housekeeper, "I don't think I ought to let you in because I've been given orders not to, but I'll fetch Miss Taylor if you'll wait here a minute."

"Please be as quick as you can," said Nick, who was afraid that Mr Barton might come back at any moment.

The housekeeper disappeared. She was away for a long time, it seemed to the children. Then at last she appeared again, this time with Miss Taylor, who was frowning. "What do you want?" she asked.

"Miss Taylor, please can we speak to you for a minute in private?" asked Nick. "We've got important news for you."

The Dragon looked hard at Nick. "About Kit, do you mean?" she said.

Nick nodded. Miss Taylor beckoned them to come inside. "Mr Barton will be back soon," she said. "You can tell him, too."

"No," said Nick, "we can't. He's working for Kit's wicked uncle!"

"What!" said the Dragon in the greatest astonishment. "Now what in the world do you know about wicked uncles and Mr Barton?"

"We know an awful lot," said Nick. "Please take us somewhere private. It's very, very important."

"Do you know where Kit is?" said the Dragon in a low tone.

Nick nodded again. Miss Taylor led them all into a little room and shut the door. Russet went in too and ran round, sniffing.

"Now what is all this mystery?" asked the Dragon, sitting down. "Begin at the beginning and tell me."

So Nick began at the very beginning and told his story. The Dragon was good at listening and did not interrupt once. Only when she learned what a traitor Mr Barton was did she move. Then she got up and walked once round the room, her face grim.

Nick went on with his tale to the very end. When at last he stopped he saw, to his great surprise, that there were tears in the Dragon's eyes!

"Poor Kit!" she said. "Poor boy!"

The children stared at her, astonished. Not one of them had ever dreamed for a moment that the fierce Dragon could shed tears! She got out her handkerchief and mopped her eyes.

"I think you're very clever, brave children!" she said. "I really do. I am glad you've come to tell me!"

Nick opened his mouth to say something but at that moment there came such a terrific hammering on the front door that everyone jumped.

"Now who's that?" said the Dragon, astonished. "What a noise to make!"

The children hoped it wasn't Mr Barton coming back! They heard the housekeeper almost running to the door. They heard the door opening and a loud American voice say something, and then a frightened-looking maid came into the room and spoke to the Dragon.

"Miss Taylor, there's a gentleman here who says he's got to see Master Kit. I said he wasn't here, but he won't believe me."

Footsteps sounded down the polished hall, and a man came in at the door. He was the same man who had spoken to Nick in the ice-cream shop, the one Nick had been rude to. He was looking worried and angry.

The Dragon leaped up from her seat. "Peter!" she said in a half-choked voice. "Peter! It can't be you!"

The man looked at her, and his face creased into affectionate, smiling lines. "Why, Jane Taylor!" he said. "So it's you who's had charge of Kit!"

"Peter! We thought you were dead!" said the Dragon, and she began to cry again. "I feel I'm in a dream. I don't understand what's happening!"

"Cheer up, Jane!" said the tall man with a laugh that sounded very much like Kit's. "I'm not dead. I never was! I wasn't in that plane that was burned out. I'd had a crash somewhere else, flying with Roy, my friend. We were both taken to the hospital, badly burned from blazing fuel, and no one knew who we were. I didn't know what was going on for months."

"Oh, Peter! Is this really all true?" said the Dragon, smiling through her tears.

"Quite true," said the man. "When I came to my senses again and realised who I was, I remembered I had a boy called Kit! And then I heard that that wicked fellow Paul had kidnapped him twice for his money. So I lay low, meaning to get him if I could. I knew Kit had been shipped off to England in charge of two people my aunt said she trusted. Then I heard Paul had gone to England, too, and I guessed why. He was after Kit again! So along I came to look for Paul, and to find Kit once more."

"Oh no! And we put you off properly," said Nick with a groan. "We thought you were Kit's wicked uncle, but – but – you're his father, aren't you?"

"I am!" said the tall man. "And I want to see Kit. Where is he?"

"At the moment he's not here," said

Nick. "He's on a houseboat we know, in a backwater up the river. We hid him there when we knew his wicked uncle was after him."

It was a pity that Nick spoke in such a loud voice, for at that moment Mr Barton was walking in at the front door! He had let himself in with his key, and he overheard what Nick was saying.

He stopped still in amazement. Then without a sound, he walked out of the front door again and made his way to the garage. So Kit was actually on the houseboat! Those children had hidden him in the very place that his enemies had planned. What a bit of luck!

"I'll go straight to Paul and tell him his parcel has arrived!" thought Mr Barton with a hard smile as he started up the car. "And we'll both go and look at the parcel together! Ha, young Kit, you're in for trouble now!"

And so Mr Barton drove off in the darkening night, not knowing that Kit's father had arrived, alive and well, ready to find his son and take him into safe-keeping as soon as he could!

Chapter 24

KIT HAS A WONDERFUL IDEA

The children and Miss Taylor had no idea that Mr Barton had overheard Nick's words. They went on talking eagerly, telling Kit's father the whole story. He listened as if he couldn't believe his ears.

"Gee!" he said. "You beat everything, you three! Tunnelling under the fence like that, climbing up the tree to the attic and taking Kit to the houseboat! You've been pretty good friends to him, I'll say you have!"

"Don't you think we ought to go and tell Kit you've arrived?" said Nick, going red with pleasure at so much praise. "For one thing, he oughtn't to be on the houseboat longer than we can help, now we know it's the hiding place his enemies had arranged for him. They might go and find him when he's asleep! And, for another thing, he'll be wild with delight when he sees you again, Mr Armstrong!"

"I'll just go and have a word with the police first," said Mr Armstrong in a very grim tone. "I've a feeling that Mr Barton, Paul and whatever other friends they've got will be better locked up in an English prison before they do any more damage. I'll get the police to surround the house they're in, and you can take me by water to the houseboat. Then, if the men try to escape, they'll find all their paths are blocked! The police will be on land and I'll be on the water!"

Mr Armstrong went off to telephone. The Dragon hugged all the children hard, one by one, much to their surprise. She seemed suddenly much younger and didn't look at all fierce.

"Things are coming right!" she said. "Dear Kit! What a wonderful surprise he'll get!"

"I wonder what he's doing now," said Nick. "I say, wasn't it a good thing Mr Barton didn't come back while all this was happening? He's been a long time posting his letter!"

Mr Barton had reached Kit's uncle by then. He poured out to the surprised man what he had overheard Nick saying. "The boy's actually on your houseboat!" he said. "Those children you turned off must be the ones that live next door to us. They made friends with Kit, got to know his secret, and for some reason have hidden him on the houseboat!"

"We'll go and see," said Paul. "What a bit of luck for us, if so! I suppose he couldn't have been there when we went to visit the boat this morning? No, we didn't see a sign of him."

"Come along quietly," said Mr Barton, setting off down the lawn to the river. "Don't say a word, or it will warn him we're about. We'll take him by surprise and that boy will feel very sorry for himself in a little while! We can't use the boat as a hiding place now, unfortunately, because those children know all about it. But it shouldn't be difficult to find somewhere else."

The men went silently down the lawn towards the willow trees that hid the boat. Kit didn't hear them. He had felt bored and, having finished his book, he was watching some rabbits playing on the twilit lawn, peering at them between the weeping willows. So, although he didn't hear the two men coming, he suddenly caught sight of them! He took a look at their faces, and his heart began to beat fast. Both men looked pleased and determined, as if they knew Kit was there! Could they possibly know?

Kit took another look at their faces, and made up his mind he wasn't going to hide on the *Black Swan*. No! He didn't feel that would be safe at all. Once these men began to make a thorough search, he would easily be found!

The boy went to the other side of the boat and slid quietly down the hull to the water. He entered it with hardly a splash. The backwater was not deep, and he could just stand on the bottom of the stream. If he kept perfectly still, no one could possibly know he was there.

The men came up to the boat very quietly indeed. They stood listening for a moment, and then parted the willows for a peep. They could see nobody, of course.

"He must be down in the cabins," whispered Mr Barton. "That's good. We can pounce on him and catch him easily there. You go that side. I'll go this."

The two men went stealthily to the door of the cabin. No one moved. They stood outside the cabin door and spoke loudly.

"Are you there, Kit?"

No answer.

"It's no good not answering," said Mr Barton, beginning to lose his temper. "We know you're there. The boy next door told us!"

Still no answer. "We'll go in and get him," said Paul impatiently. "Come on!"

They both went in. There seemed to be no one in the cabins at all. The men began to strip the bunks and search everywhere for the boy they thought was hiding.

And it was then that the Great Idea came to Kit!

It was such a wonderful idea that he could hardly climb up the side of the boat because he was trembling so much with excitement. He swung himself silently on to the deck and, keeping himself well out of sight, he crept round to the door that led to the cabins. He felt for the padlock and slipped it into place. Then, with a quick movement, he swung the strong new door shut, turned the key in the lock, and fastened the padlock too, so that the door was shut fast and doubly locked.

The men heard the bang of the door. Mr Barton leaped to open it, but the key turned before he could jerk it open. Then he heard the padlock rattling against the door.

"Who's there?" shouted Mr Barton, hammering on the door. "Let us out!"

"It's me, Kit!" said Kit. "You wanted to make me a prisoner, didn't you? Well, how does it feel? I hope you'll find the cabins big enough for you!"

The men looked to see if they could smash the windows and get out, but the frames were far too small for grown men to squeeze through. They really were prisoners! Mr Barton completely lost his temper and began to bang on the door as if he were mad.

"Shut up!" said Kit's uncle to him. "You're making too much noise. Let me talk to Kit."

But Kit was not in the mood to listen to anything that his uncle said to him. He sat out on the deck, his heart beating fast, rejoicing because he had so neatly captured his two enemies. Now, if only Nick would come and see him, how surprised he would be!

"I'll wait till Nick comes," thought Kit. "He's sure to come tonight. Then I'll send him back to phone the police. I'll keep guard on Mr Barton and my uncle till the police come. What a row they're making! I hope they don't break down the door!"

It was a good thing the houseboat was so far from the house, or the other man and the caretaker would most certainly have heard the shouting and hammering of the two angry prisoners. Kit felt a little anxious as he remembered the strength of the two men. They had, after all, broken in the door of the playroom. If they went on like this, they might be able to free themselves. Still, it was getting dark now, so he could easily escape in the darkness and hide somewhere. He wasn't at all afraid but he did badly want those men to remain his prisoners till Nick came. It had been a wonderful idea to lock them in!

Kit sat quietly on the deck, watching the night darken the water. He strained his ears to hear any boat coming. He did so long for Nick to arrive. Maybe the Dragon would come too. Wouldn't she laugh to see the surly Mr Barton locked up in the cabin with Kit's wicked uncle!

Kit suddenly pricked up his ears like a dog. He was sure he had heard the distant sound of oars. It was getting so dark now that he couldn't see very far. He strained his eyes, trying to make out any boat coming up the backwater.

Then suddenly he saw one, looming up out of the shadows. There seemed to be a lot of people in it, and one was a man. Kit sat tight and made no sound. He was not at all sure whether this boatful of people contained his friends! Suppose they were strangers, come for an evening picnic? They might hear the shouting and hammering of the two prisoners, and insist on letting them out! Kit decided to sit quietly and say nothing at all, and hope the boatload would go by, if it was made up of strangers. They certainly would not see the *Black Swan* hidden in the willows.

Just then the prisoners did start shouting again. The people in the boat stopped rowing for a moment, and then slid quietly up the backwater and past the houseboat.

Then suddenly Kit felt someone pouncing on him fiercely, taking firm hold of his shoulders, and shaking him like a rat!

"I've got one of them!" shouted a voice. "Bring a torch, quick!"

Chapter 25

Good News for Kit

After Kit's father had gone to phone the police, the children sat waiting with the Dragon. Mr Armstrong soon came back, a broad smile on his face.

"The police were most interested in what I had to tell them," he said. "They're going to the house you described, and I said we'd go round by the river, and prevent the men from escaping that way. You'd better come with me, Nick, because I shan't know the right way."

"We're coming, too," said Katie, and Laura nodded her head.

"No, not you girls," said Nick.

"Why not?" asked Katie fiercely. "You've had all the fun lately. We haven't had any. We're coming too."

"I'll come as well, to keep the girls company," said the Dragon, unexpectedly. "I really feel as if I must see Kit as soon as possible. Shall we go up the river now, Peter? It's getting rather dark."

"Yes, we must go straight away," said Mr Armstrong. "Come along. Lead the way, Nick."

So Nick led the way down the drive into his own garden, down to the bottom, and across the fields to the river.

He found the boat, and everyone got in. Nick untied the rope and pushed off. The little boat seemed quite crowded with five people and one dog because, of course, Russet had come too. He wasn't going to be left out of anything.

"I hope we find Kit safe and well," said Mr Armstrong anxiously. "I hate to think of him under the very nose of those evil people. They might find him at any moment."

"Kit will be all right!" said Nick. "He's really a very clever boy, Mr Armstrong. Oh, dear, I'm awfully sorry I was rude to you that day in the ice-cream shop! But, you see, I was on the lookout for Kit's wicked uncle, and I really thought you were him, snooping round, asking questions."

"That's all right!" said Mr Armstrong,

rowing strongly up the river. "You did put me off, of course. I felt sure there was no boy hiding anywhere in Faldham. I thought I'd got hold of the wrong place, and went off to another Faldham. But I soon found that my first address was right, and came back to it, as you saw."

"I suppose it's you who's rich now, and not Kit?" said Laura.

"Quite right," said Mr Armstrong. "But Paul won't find it quite so easy to kidnap me!"

"Now we're passing our little island," said Katie, peering through the twilight. "We shall soon be opposite the lonely house, where the houseboat used to be."

"Don't speak loudly then," said Kit's father. "Sounds carry a long way over water, you know, and we don't want to warn the men of our arrival, if they're anywhere about."

So nobody said a word more for some time. They passed the place where the houseboat had originally been moored, and went on to where the little backwater began. It was difficult to see in the twilight. But Nick knew his way well by now and guided the boat deftly into it.

"Where's the houseboat?" whispered Mr Armstrong.

"Hidden in that enormous pair of willow trees," whispered back Nick. "You can only just see them. Hey, what's that?"

It was a noise of shouting! It seemed to come from the houseboat. Then there came a tremendous hammering. Mr Armstrong stopped rowing at once and they all listened.

"Mr Armstrong! I believe they've got Kit locked up in the cabins!" whispered Nick in dismay. "That's somebody shouting for help, though it's rather muffled and it really does sound as if someone's hammering on the door trying to get out. Oh, I do hope Kit is all right!"

"I think I'll take the boat quietly past the houseboat and moor it a little way up," said Kit's father. "It's quite likely they've left somebody on guard on deck and, if so, we don't want to warn them we're here. Now, not a word from anyone!"

Very quietly indeed, with hardly a splash from the oars, the boat slipped by the houseboat, keeping towards the opposite side of the backwater. Mr Armstrong rowed some way past, and then turned into the bank. The nose of the boat pushed into the long grass, and Kit's father leaped out. He felt about for a tree trunk, and tied the boat to it.

"Nick, you can come with me," he whispered. "The girls must stay here with Miss Taylor. Now, don't make any noise at all."

The man and the boy crept over the grass towards the big willow trees in which the houseboat was hidden. When they got to the boat, Kit's father peered on to the deck.

"There's someone sitting there!" he whispered. "Somebody on guard, I should think. Well, I'll pounce on him and overpower him and then we'll rescue Kit."

He didn't know it was Kit himself sitting there quietly, keeping guard over the two men, who were now quiet again in the cabins! He crept forward on to the deck of the boat, so silently that Kit didn't hear a sound. Then, with a quick leap, his strong arms were round the surprised boy, pinning him so tightly that he couldn't move!

"I've got one of them!" he shouted to Nick. "Bring a torch, quick!"

"Hey! Let me go!" roared Kit, trying to struggle. He thought it must be one of the men from the house. He fought furiously, but the man's grip was too tight for him to escape. He shouted out:

"Let me go! Let me go!"

Nick knew Kit's voice at once, and he yelled to Mr Armstrong. "That's Kit! Let him go!"

But with Kit shouting too, Mr Armstrong didn't hear what Nick yelled, and he held Kit in an iron grip. Then, feeling that he was small, he let go one hand and felt round for Nick's torch. He switched it on to see whom he had caught.

The light fell right on Kit's angry face. Mr Armstrong stared down in amazement. Why, it was Kit, his own son! He gave a shout of joy.

"Kit! It's you, old son! Are you all right? Oh, Kit, I've found you at last!"

Kit's heart beat loudly. It was his father's voice, which he had once known so well! But how could it be? His father was dead. Nick leaped on board and spoke to Kit.

"Kit! It's your father! It really is! He called on the Dragon tonight. He wasn't killed in that plane crash. He's alive!"

Kit stood up, and father and son faced one another in the remaining twilight. Kit flung his arms round his father's waist and buried his head in his shoulder.

"Dad!" he said with a choke in his voice. "I can't believe it!"

"It's true, old son!" said his father, patting him on the back. "My word, I didn't know it was you when I jumped on you just now! I thought you were yelling down in those cabins!"

The shouting and hammering began again. Nick looked towards Kit. "Who's there?" he asked, in surprise.

"Mr Barton and my dear Uncle Paul," said Kit proudly. "They came back again. I waited till they had gone into the cabins, and then I hopped up and locked them in – using the same padlock they had hoped to use for me!"

"Good for you!" said Nick, delighted. "It's great to think of those two captured. That's brilliant!"

"I think we'll go and see if the police have arrived yet," said Mr Armstrong, still with an arm round Kit. "I phoned them some time ago. I don't feel quite capable of capturing two madmen on my own!"

"I'll just slip along and tell Miss Taylor and the girls what we're going to do," said Nick, who knew that Katie and Laura would complain bitterly at being left out of the fun again if he didn't go to them. "Shan't be long. I'll join you later. I know the way to the house."

Nick sped back to the girls, and Mr Armstrong and Kit made their way to the house to see if by any chance the police had arrived yet. Nick told the girls in a few words how clever Kit had been.

"And there those two men are, captured as neatly as anything!" he finished. "Isn't Kit great?"

But just as he spoke a tremendous noise came from the houseboat. The two men were making one last bid for freedom, and with their combined strength were hurling themselves against the door. It broke from its hinges and went flying back, hanging by the lock!

"They're out!" yelled Nick, and ran for the houseboat, though what he was going to do, he didn't know! He couldn't stop the men, that was obvious!

The two men ran for cover. They knew it wouldn't be safe to go back to the house. They plunged into the bushes, and were soon well hidden. Not a sound was to be heard. It was really infuriating!

"Oh, I do hope they won't get away!" said Nick. "Who's that? Laura, go back to the boat at once."

"I've brought Russet," said Laura. "He'll smell out the two men if I tell him to. Oh, look! Is that the police?"

It was. Three men were coming down the lawn with Mr Armstrong and Kit. They hailed the others.

"Hi! What was that noise we heard?"

"The men escaped," said Nick, groaning. "They're in the bushes somewhere. It'll be impossible to try and find them in the dark."

"Russet! Go and find rabbits, big rabbits!" said Laura to the eager spaniel. "Hurry now!"

Russet shot off. He felt certain that Laura meant him to find the men who had just run off. He put his nose to the ground and followed the scent of the men. Russet would find them if anyone could!

Chapter 26

BACK HOME AGAIN – AND A BIRTHDAY PARTY

Everyone stood still, waiting for the dog to bark. Suddenly they heard him: "Woof, woof, woof! Woof, woof, woof!"

"He's found them!" said Laura, pleased. "Good old Russet!"

The police made their way to the barking dog. He was standing a little way from a thick bush and barking at it. The police saw the grass had been trampled round about, and guessed that the men were there.

"Come out of your own accord, or we'll probe for you with sticks," warned the inspector. There was a moment's silence, and then the two men crawled out, looking very sulky in the light of the police torches.

"I think we'll go back to the house," said the inspector. "Take these men, constables."

The two policemen each took charge of a

prisoner, and the whole company went up the lawn to the house. The old caretaker was there, and she stared in the utmost astonishment when she saw everyone coming in.

"What next?" she said. "Whatever next? This beats everything! I'll give my notice in tomorrow, so I will!"

But nobody took any notice of her. The two policemen swung the prisoners round to face the inspector and then Kit's uncle gave a loud cry. He had suddenly seen Kit's father.

"Peter!" he cried. "No, it can't be Peter! But if it's not, who is it? Peter's dead!"

"No, he's not dead," said Mr Armstrong, in a quiet and very cold voice. "He's very much alive and kicking. And he's going to have a reckoning with you, Paul, for your treatment of his son!"

Paul went pale. He might have been able to lie his way out of trouble with the others, but he could not deceive Kit's own father, who had known him and his bad ways for years. He was his stepbrother, and had turned to crime when he was a young man. He lowered his eyes and said nothing.

"As for you," said Kit's father, turning to Mr Barton. "You are a rat and a worm! To take charge of a boy, and accept payment for that charge, and then to bargain with his uncle for his capture! I can tell you, I shall not rest until you have a fit punishment. You will certainly never be allowed to teach children again."

Mr Barton could think of nothing to say. He had never been kind to Kit, so he couldn't expect the boy to say a good word for him. His wicked ways had found him out at last. He stood there, surly and sulky, giving the Dragon a hard look now and again.

"Well, I'll take charge of these men now," said the inspector, nodding to the two policemen to take them away. "We've got a car outside. Perhaps you'll see me again in the morning, Mr Armstrong? Thank you."

Mr Barton and Kit's uncle were hustled out of the room. The children heard the front door bang and then a car door. The car engine started up and the big police car roared off into the night, taking the two kidnappers to prison.

"That's the end of them," said Katie,

with a sigh of relief. "Oh, Kit – aren't you glad to see your father?"

"I should just think I am!" said Kit, who had not left his father's side once. He couldn't believe he was really there. It was wonderful.

Katie yawned. "Time you were in bed," said the Dragon. "Come along. We must all go back."

"I'll just have a word with the old caretaker," said Mr Armstrong. "The poor thing can't make out what's happening."

"There was another man here once," said Nick, suddenly remembering.

"Well, we'll be able to get him, too, I've no doubt," said Mr Armstrong. He went to speak to the old woman, and she grumbled away at him, shaking her head.

"Nice goings-on, these are! I'm right glad Mr Cunningham's back from abroad. He ought to know about all this, so he ought!"

"Don't you worry, I'll call him," said Mr Armstrong. "What's his number, please?"

Soon Kit's father was talking to Mr Cunningham, who was very surprised to hear what had been happening on the

Black Swan since he had left.

"I'll come over tomorrow," he promised. "We'll meet on the houseboat, shall we? Dear me, I've just remembered that it's my birthday. Tell Laura I'll bring a cake, not so nice as hers perhaps, but still quite nice. We'll eat it, and drink lemonade at eleven o'clock."

"Isn't he kind?" said the children, looking at one another. "Hey! Maybe we can have the *Black Swan* properly for ourselves again now!"

They went back home in the little boat, sleepy, excited and tired. Laura's mother was home by this time, feeling very worried and anxious to find none of the children about. In all the excitement they had forgotten to leave her a note. She was even more surprised to see Kit and his father, and the Dragon, too!

"What is all this?" she cried.

"Oh, Aunt Marion! Do you remember hearing about a boy called Sam, who was dumb?" cried Nick. "Well, here he is."

"How do you do?" said Kit, holding out his hand.

"He's not dumb!" said Laura's mother.

Everyone laughed. Then they settled down to a good old talk, and Mrs Greyling listened in growing amazement.

"To think all this has been happening under my very nose and I didn't know a thing!" she said, half indignantly. "Well, well, it's a good thing everything has come right. You might have got yourselves and Kit into serious trouble."

"Oh, no, Mrs Greyling, children like yours get other people out of trouble," said Mr Armstrong, with a laugh. "Now, I'm going to take Kit off to bed. He's tired out. Goodnight, children. See you tomorrow!"

The Dragon, Mr Armstrong and Kit went to their house next door, and Mrs Greyling bundled three excited children up to bed.

"I'll never got to sleep!" said Katie. "I want to talk till midnight!"

But they were all asleep in a few minutes, and didn't wake till breakfast time the next morning.

"It's Mr Cunningham's birthday party today," said Laura to the others. "I hope he has a nice cake! Won't it be fun to tell him everything?"

They were all on the *Black Swan* at eleven o'clock. Mr Cunningham was already there, looking as twinkly as ever. On a table was the biggest birthday cake the children had ever seen. It was really enormous and had pink-and-white icing all over it.

"Now," said Mr Cunningham, "who will have a slice of my birthday cake with me? Nick, get the lemonade, will you? I've put it all in a bucket of ice to keep cool, down in the cabin."

What a feast that was! Enormous slices of the creamiest cake the children had ever eaten, washed down with iced lemonade, so cold that it made their throats hurt when they swallowed. But, as Laura said, it was "a very nice sort of hurt!"

Mr Cunningham heard all the story through from start to finish, and inspected the door that had been broken down the night before.

"That's the only damage these children have caused," he said solemnly to Mr Armstrong. "Very nice children, these. In fact, I'm thinking of selling my boat to them."

"What do you mean, Mr Cunningham?" asked Nick at last.

"Well," said Mr Cunningham. "I don't want the boat, you know, and you certainly seem to have found a lot of use for it, keeping men prisoner and so on, and I think it would be a good thing if I sold it to you."

"Well, sir, we'd simply love to buy it, but how much do you want for it?" asked Nick eagerly. "We haven't got very much money saved up at present. But I've got some in the bank."

"I don't want much for it," said Mr Cunningham. "I'm coming back to live in my house here, you know. So, if you would like to buy the *Black Swan*, I would be willing to sell it to you on your promise of paying me at least fifty-two visits a year! Is that too much, do you think?"

The children had been expecting him to say fifty-two pounds. They stared at him, delighted. "But that's not proper payment," said Laura at last. "A visit isn't a payment. We'd visit you for nothing."

"Pardon me, but you do pay calls, and visits," said Mr Cunningham solemnly.

"And that's the payment I'd like. Is it a bargain?"

"Oh, yes!" cried Katie joyfully. It would be lovely to go and see Mr Cunningham once a week, he was so nice. And what fun to have the *Black Swan* for their very own, to play on each holiday and to sleep in whenever they liked.

"Is Kit to share it, too?" asked Katie.

"Of course," said Mr Cunningham. "Though I suppose he will be going back to America with his father soon, won't he?"

"He'll stay for the rest of the holidays," said Mr Armstrong, and the children gave a whoop of delight. "I'd like to see a bit of England now I'm here. And, Mr Cunningham, I'd be very happy if you'd pay me a visit whenever you're in America."

It was a very happy morning. Everyone had two slices of birthday cake each, even Russet, and as much lemonade as they could drink. Then they said goodbye to Mr Cunningham and promised to visit him again as soon as they could.

"Don't you get behind with your payments!" he called as they went off in the boat.

"We won't!" cried all the children, and waved wildly at him.

"Well, I'm quite sorry that adventure's over," said Nick.

"I'm not," said Kit. "Oh, Dad, it's lovely to have you back again. I can't believe it's true!"

"It's true all right," said his father, and smiled at the boy beside him. "We're going to have some fun together, Kit, you see if we don't!"

"And we've got the old *Black Swan* for our very own!" cried Laura, remembering. "Aren't we lucky!"

"We'll have wonderful times on her," said Katie.

And there's no doubt about it – they certainly will!

Enid Blyton

THE YOUNG ADVENTURERS

Read all about the exciting adventures of
Nick, Katie, Laura and their friends.

ISBN 978-1-84135-737-9

ISBN 978-1-84135-738-6

ISBN 978-1-84135-739-3

ISBN 978-1-84135-740-9

ISBN 978-1-84135-741-6

ISBN 978-1-84135-742-3

Enid Blyton

THE ADVENTUROUS FOUR

Follow the adventures of Tom, twins Pippa
and Zoe, and their friend Andy who has a sailing
boat on which the four love to go exploring.

ISBN 978-1-84135-734-8

ISBN 978-1-84135-735-5

ISBN 978-1-84135-736-2

Enid Blyton

THE BARNEY MYSTERIES

Join Barney, Roger, Diana and Snubby
on their mystery-solving adventures!

ISBN 978-1-84135-728-7

ISBN 978-1-84135-729-4

ISBN 978-1-84135-730-0

ISBN 978-1-84135-731-7

ISBN 978-1-84135-732-4

ISBN 978-1-84135-733-1

Enid Blyton

The Secret Series

Follow the adventures of Mike, Peggy and
Nora as they discover a secret island, explore
the heart of Africa and unravel the mysteries of
the Killimooin Mountains...

PB ISBN 978-1-84135-673-0
HB ISBN 978-1-84135-748-5

PB ISBN 978-1-84135-675-4
HB ISBN 978-1-84135-749-2

PB ISBN 978-1-84135-676-1
HB ISBN 978-1-84135-750-8

PB ISBN 978-1-84135-677-8
HB ISBN 978-1-84135-751-5

PB ISBN 978-1-84135-674-7
HB ISBN 978-1-84135-752-2

PB ISBN 978-1-84135-678-5
HB ISBN 978-1-84135-753-9

Enid Blyton

Family
Adventures

ISBN 978-1-84135-645-7

ISBN 978-1-84135-646-4

ISBN 978-1-84135-647-1

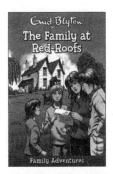

ISBN 978-1-84135-648-8

ISBN 978-1-84135-649-5

ISBN 978-1-84135-650-1

Enid Blyton
ADVENTURE OMNIBUSES

ISBN 978-1-84135-588-7

As soon as Peter, Pam and their cousin Brock
hear about the strange castle by the sea they are
determined to solve its mystery, but an unknown
enemy awaits them in the castle's secret and
ghostly passages...

ISBN 978-1-84135-587-0

Bob and Mary decide to search their Granny's
house for a necklace they see in a family portrait.
But will their big cousin Ralph help or hinder them?

Enid Blyton

ADVENTURE OMNIBUSES

ISBN 978-1-84135-589-4

Discover the trials and tribulations of six cousins who are forced to share life on a country farm, how they learn to adapt their lives to suit one another, and the scrapes and adventures they have together.

Enid Blyton

Enid Blyton was born in London in 1897. Her childhood was spent in Beckenham, Kent and as a child she began to write poems, stories and plays.

She trained as a teacher, but devoted most of her life to writing for children. Her first book was a collection of poems, published in 1922. In 1926 she began to write a weekly magazine for children called _Sunny Stories_, and it was here that many of her most popular stories and characters first appeared.

She wrote more than 700 books for children, many of which have been translated into over 30 languages.